THE BUCKAROO

THE BUCKAROO

BURT ARTHUR

CUTTING EDGE

ISBN-13: 978-1-954840-51-5

Published by
Cutting Edge Books
PO Box 8212
Calabasas, CA 91372
www.cuttingedgebooks.com

CHAPTER ONE

The signpost at the entrance to the town lay wearily forward in its hole in the ground. An assortment of rocks and stones that had once helped the post fill the hole lay strewn about. A single rusted nail held the crosspiece in place on the post but it did not prevent it from pointing earthward instead of westward, in the direction of the town that lay beyond it. A lean youth astride a brown mare had stopped beside the signpost. His head cocked a bit to one side, he eyed it critically. He bent sideways in the saddle, craning his neck in an effort to read the faded lettering on the crosspiece and after a moment's futile twisting and squinting he abandoned it, straightened up, scowled darkly and muttered something as he settled himself in the saddle. Mike, his patient mare, turned her head and looked at him quizzically. She made no attempt to hurry him. She had learned long since that one had to be patient with Tad Cole if one hoped to get along with him; patience, she had discovered early in their association, saved her strength and energy as well as some slight wear and tear on her legs even if it didn't always save her from a torrid tongue-lashing when Tad had to blame someone other than himself for the mistakes he made. Yet despite her master's temperament and occasional flare-up, Mike was a rather contented mare. Of course she hadn't taken too kindly to her name. Even a horse has a certain sense of dignity, and the thoroughly male name that Tad had bestowed upon her annoyed her at times. But she was wise and she refused to permit the matter of a mere name to come between them.

Mike was not an especially good-looking horse, and she was fully aware of it. But she seemed to satisfy Tad and that was all that mattered. She was fully aware, too, of Tad's shortcomings; but she was loyal to him and on more than one occasion when some overly sympathetic horse tethered close by overheard Tad berate her, and moved closer to her to offer her a bit of comfort, Mike promptly showed how she regarded intruders by rearing up and lashing out with her hoofs so viciously that the other horse backed hastily out of range.

Mike had sense by the tone of Tad's mutterings that he was annoyed; it had been a hot and dusty ride, with the unrelenting sun overhead almost all the way, and now Tad was jaded and irritable. When he nudged her with his knees, Mike wheeled obediently and cantered townward. She could tell by the tightening pressure of his knees against her sturdy sides that he was sitting upright, an indication that he was interested in what lay about them and in what he could see directly ahead.

Tad had already noticed that the town was a typical cow town. It had but a single street and everything of importance was concentrated there. At the moment it was crowded with vehicles of all types; there were wagons and buckboards, carts and buggies, and they lined both sides of the street, making street-crossing an impossibility, save at the corners. The hitching posts, he noted too, were crowded with tied-up horses. There was a general twisting around and a craning of necks among them when Mike appeared; here and there a horse backed out from among his mates, gave Mike an appraising looking-over and whinnied a welcome. Mike's head jerked upward haughtily, or perhaps it was a coy female's reaction—at any rate, she did not acknowledge the greetings. Tad pulled her to a sudden stop when they came abreast of a crowded store doorway. Mike snorted in protest; the bit had cut into her mouth.

A couple of men on the fringe of the crowd turned and looked at Tad briefly, then as one they turned away again. There was a short, stocky man among them and he scurried about seeking an opening through which he might inch his way. But his efforts proved fruitless and presently he stopped; after a moment he stood up on his tip-toes and tried to peer over the others' heads. Again he was unsuccessful; he gave up in disgust and sank down on his heels. He took off his hat, and fanned himself. He stopped abruptly when he felt Tad's eyes on him, and he turned around and glared at him.

"Howdy," Tad said. "What's the name o' this place, partner, and what's goin' on in there?"

The little man's lip curled.

"The name of this town," he said with biting emphasis, "is Shorthorn."

"You don't say! Shorthorn, eh?"

"Yes. I don't suppose you approve of the name, but since we built the town, you must admit we have a right to call it what we like."

"Yesh, sure," Tad said quickly.

"Thank you."

"Forget it. What'd you say was goin' on in there?"

"I didn't say."

"O-h!"

"That," the man said with a nod in the direction of the store, "happens to be a court of law. You know—' place where trials are held. You're probably too young to—"

"Look, mister," Tad interrupted darkly.

"Y-es?"

Tad scowled but said nothing further; instead, he swung himself out of the saddle, draped the reins over Mike's head, leaving her to her own devices. The mare looked at him questioningly but Tad was in no mood for her. He hitched up his pants, sauntered forward, stopped alongside the stocky man.

"No room inside, eh?" Tad asked in an effort to make conversation.

"O-h, yes," the man replied. "Lots of it, as a matter of fact. We prefer it out here, though, because we like standing in the sun."

Another man turned his head. He had raggedy, turned-up mustaches and they seemed to quiver with annoyance.

"Look, partner," he said to Tad, "there's a murder trial goin' on inside, and every once in a while, 'cept when some flannel-mouthed galoot comes along and starts jawin' away, we manage to get part o' what's bein' said in there. 'Course it ain't much, but we do awright with it. Now if you've got nuthin' to do, how about you doin' it somewheres else 'stead o' here, huh?"

The stocky man grinned.

"That's an excellent suggestion, my friend," he said. "I think you ought to act on it."

Tad scowled again but he did not reply to either of them. He straightened up to his full height, stared straight ahead. Suddenly he realized that he could see into the courtroom. It was a large store, and it was crowded from wall to wall. A narrow aisle that led from the doorway to a table at the far end of the store divided the place in two. Solid rows of benches flanked the aisle but they were crowded to capacity. There were almost as many standees, and Tad glanced at them disinterestedly as his eyes ranged forward and focused on the table area. There were two men standing in front of the table, two sharply contrasting figures, a slender youth and a burly man. The latter turned at that moment, just long enough for Tad to catch a glimpse of a silver star pinned to the man's shirt front. Behind the table sat a bald-headed man with thin lips and a long nose set in a stern face. He wore silver or steel-rimmed glasses and his sharp eyes seemed to bore out at everyone. To the left of the table were the jurymen—six grave-faced men seated in two rows of threes; on the right sat a tall, slender man with gray-black hair parted in the middle. When he arose and came forward to the table, Tad heard someone say, "There's Cummings again. He's got the case clinched and the kid hangin', judgin' by the way he's struttin'. That feller's got ice water in 'is veins and a poker face t' boot."

"That kid in here," Tad breathed into the ear of the mustached man in front of him, "he the one on trial?"

The man grunted in the affirmative.

"What's he bein' tried for?" Tad asked.

"Murder," the man snapped over his shoulder. "How many times d' you hafta be told?"

"He don't look like a murderer to me," Tad said calmly.

There was a sudden movement inside the store and the crowd surged forward and swept through the doorway and into the courtroom. Those in the front of the crowd promptly darted away in search of seats. Presently they abandoned their fruitless quest and trudged off toward the walls, turning every now and then to cast black looks and mutterings over their hunched shoulders at their more fortunate townsmen who laughed at them and added insult to hurt feelings by thumbing their noses in parting. One seat-searcher failed to watch his step and tripped over a suddenly thrust-out foot. He sprawled on his face amid howls of laughter. No one offered to help him up and he finally managed to get up by himself; as he turned away for the second time, someone scaled his hat after him. It caromed off his head and he whirled around angrily; a gavel banged loudly on the table and he picked up his hat and slunk off toward the rear. Tad had found an opening against a wall; he forced himself into the space just as someone tripped over his feet. His hands shot out, gripped the man, steadied him. It was the stocky man and Tad grinned down at him.

"Hi," Tad said.

"Hi, yourself," the man retorted. Tad pulled him back against the wall.

"That feller sitting behind the table," Tad said. "He looks mean enough to eat nails. He the judge?"

"Yes," came the reply, a guarded, low-voiced answer. "His name's Bailey and if he catches you talking, he'll slap a ten-dollar fine on you so fast you'll never know what hit you."

"If he can find ten bucks on me," Tad whispered, "I'll divide with him. S-ay, Shorty—"

"The name's Cahill," the stocky man hissed.

"That's better than Shorthorn," Tad whispered. "Who'd the kid murder?"

"O-h, a couple of eccentric characters. The Hassett brothers, Abe and Judd."

Tad's eyebrows arched.

"Two o' them," he mused. "He don't believe in doin' things by halves, does he?"

"Evidently not," Cahill responded out of the corner of his mouth. "Still, Shorthorn won't suffer any great loss by their sudden, and I suppose I should add, untimely departure. However, there's the law to be reckoned with, and now young Curly Walker's going to hang for breaking it. Of course, if he and his folks weren't homesteaders, things would have been different. He'd even have been supplied with an attorney. But you know how cattlemen feel about homesteaders, don't you?"

"I've got an idea," Tad said briefly. "But how come no lawyer for the kid?"

Cahill's eyes gleamed.

"The powers that be in Shorthorn saw to that," he replied significantly.

Tad nodded understandingly.

Cummings had been standing facing the spectators. That he was annoyed with them, and impatient, too, was evident, judging by the expression on his face. The gavel pounded again. As the crowd settled back and quieted down, Cummings turned slowly to face Judge Bailey.

"Yes, Mr. Prosecutor?" the judge asked.

"Will the court charge the jury, please?"

Bailey nodded, turned in his chair.

"Gentlemen of the jury," he began in a crisp tone. The six men seated on his left sat stiffly erect in their chairs. "You have heard the state's witness testify that they saw the defendant, Abel Walker, lurking about in the vicinity of the murdered men's homes. You have heard the sheriff and others, all reputable citizens of the community, testify to the effect that the defendant's clothes were bloodstained, and that certain articles found upon his person were later identified as having belonged to the deceased. Finally, testimony established the motive for the crimes as robbery."

Judge Bailey paused, coughed lightly behind his hand.

"This court," he went on again shortly, "must admit that the defendant's guilt has been established. However, it is up to you, gentlemen of the jury, to determine the degree of guilt. If you believe that Abel Walker planned to rob the Hassetts, but that he did not plan to do them bodily harm, then you will find him guilty of second-degree murder. In view of the testimony presented here, this court does not subscribe to that theory. If you believe, and the evidence does not permit you to believe otherwise, that Abel Walker planned to kill the Hassett brothers, and then to rob them, you will find him guilty of murder in the first degree. However, in view of the defendant's youth, should you recommend consideration for him, this court would be inclined to accept such a recommendation and act accordingly. Have you any questions?"

The first man of the six raised his hand.

Tad felt a tug at his shirt sleeve and he bent his head.

"That polecat's Jess Vaughn," Cahill whispered in his ear. "He's just about the meanest, nastiest man in the county. I'd rather see them hang him than that boy."

"Yes?" Judge Bailey asked.

"Judge," Vaughn inquired, "does first d'gree murder mean a hangin'?"

"The death penalty is mandatory in first-degree murder. The law is very definite on that point," Bailey replied. "Does the jury wish to confer in private?"

Vaughn shook his head.

"We've done all the c'nferrin' we need to," he said.

"I see," the judge said. "Then am I to assume that you have already arrived at a verdict?"

Vaughn nodded grimly.

"Foreman of the jury," Bailey ordered, "please rise."

Vaughn climbed to his feet. He was a tall, gaunt man, over six feet in height.

"How do you find?"

"We find the defend'nt guilty o' murder in the first d'gree," Vaughn droned.

"Any recommendations?"

Jess Vaughn looked down at the men sitting beside him.

"Nope," he said determinedly. "No recommendations."

The judge turned away and Vaughn sat down again.

"Prisoner at the bar," Bailey said and the youth standing in front of him jerked his head up. "Have you anything to say before sentence is pronounced?"

"No-no, sir," Tad heard a boyish voice say tremulously. "Nothing 'cept I didn't do it."

Vaughn laughed out loud. When Judge Bailey's gavel thumped, the gaunt juror stiffened and frowned, coughed behind his hand.

"Prisoner at the bar," the judge said again, "you have been found guilty of murder in the first degree. You are hereby sentenced to be hanged by the neck till you are dead. Execution tomorrow morning at sunup. Sheriff, take the prisoner away."

The burly lawman took the youth by the arm; slowly they moved away from the table, started up the aisle toward the door. Every head in the courtroom turned, every eye in the place followed them. They were halfway up the aisle when a lithe figure clad in dungarees and jacket, and the blondest hair that Tad ever seen bound up in a red ribbon, appeared in the doorway. He gulped when he saw a big Colt gleam in her right hand.

"Curly!" she cried.

The prisoner squirmed out of his captor's grasp, whirled away from him, stumbled and nearly fell, then retaining his feet somehow, came plunging up the aisle. A man sprang to his feet, trampled some of his neighbors as he pushed into the aisle. He thrust out one hand with which to seize the boy, reached for his gun with the other hand. Young Walker was barely a step away from him when Tad leaped between them, hurled himself at the man, struck him full tilt and sent him reeling backward. There was a howl of pain, a curse, when the man trod on those nearest him; finally he fell among them. A bench crashed over to add to the din and the girl in the doorway, forgotten for the moment, found herself rendered helpless. She raised her gun, checked herself, snapped it upward again only to lower it a second time when she found herself unable to do anything in the ever-increasing excitement and confusion. It was Curly who solved her difficulty by flashing past Tad and out the door.

There was a bellow of rage behind Tad and he twisted away instinctively as the sheriff lunged for him. Other hands reached for him, too, clutched at him, tore at his shirt as they sought to grab him. He struck wildly, madly, landed squarely on a man's face, felt bone crunch beneath his fists, cleared a path for himself to the doorway.

"Come on!" a voice cried to him and he turned to find the girl at his side. "Come on!"

He needed no further urging. They burst out of the place together, merged into the bright sunlight. The girl, evidently assuming that Tad would follow her, raced up the street. Fifty feet away she stopped, looked back, motioned frantically to Tad but before he could do anything in response, Mike crowded against him and Tad flung himself astride her, wheeled her while he was still in motion, and sent her pounding away. There were shots behind him and a roar of rifle and pistol fire. A bullet whined past his head and he promptly threw himself forward, clung to Mike's mane with both hands. Ahead of him men poured into the street and he wondered where they had come from; some of them fired at him but there was haste and bad aiming in their shooting. Then at the corner a man with a half-raised rifle in his hands blocked their way. The man shouted something but it was lost in the deafening din of hoofs, shots and shouts; he threw up his rifle and fired. Mike screamed in mingled terror and fury. She swerved suddenly, headed directly for the man. There was another scream; it echoed the length of the street, lingered in the air above the din.

Presently they were thundering out of Shorthorn. They flashed past the leaning signpost. Tad pulled himself up into the saddle, glanced back over his shoulder. He caught a fleeting glimpse of a band of riders straining to shorten the gap between him and themselves and he whacked Mike across the flank with his open hand, sent the mare bounding away. There were scattered shots and he disregarded them. When a stray bullet slithered the roadway between Mike's pounding hoofs, Tad swore in a yell, jerked out his gun, turned around and snapped a leaden answer. He saw a lead horse plunge to his knees and send his rider sailing over his head: the man landed on his shoulder and crashed over as limply as a felled tree. A second horse, limping badly, was pulled away to the side of the road. Tad grunted, indicating that he was satisfied. Scornfully he turned his back on his pursuers, holstered his gun and settled himself in the saddle. It was his way of telling Mike that the rest of the job was hers. It was up to her to lose their pursuers. Mike seemed to sense it in the pressure of Tad's knees against her sides. Instantly she lengthened her stride and when Tad glanced backward again casually, the pursuing horsemen were far behind. He leaned forward, patted Mike's sweaty neck.

"Good girl," he said and Mike's pounding hoofs echoed her answer.

Fifteen minutes later there was no sign whatever of the revenge-seeking citizens of Shorthorn. He checked Mike's furious pace, slowed her down to a canter. It was a short time after that when he happened to look up and spied a motionless figure astride an idling horse filling the roadway about a hundred yards ahead of them. Instinctively Mike stiffened. Tad frowned, eyed and studied the figure while his right hand stole downward and tightened around the butt of his gun. He grunted, relaxed, when he recognized the rider. Mike sensed that the threat of danger was passed, and she eased herself, too. It was the girl with the red ribbon wound around her blond hair. They were still some twenty or thirty feet away when she wheeled her mount, twisted around and beckoned to him.

"Follow me!" she cried, spurred her horse and loped away southward.

Tad nudged Mike with his knees. The mare snorted but she quickened her pace without delay. The girl swung off the road, pulled up for a moment until she was satisfied that Tad was following her, then she rode on again. Mike put on an added burst of speed, clattered up to the spot only to see the girl ride down an incline. Tad jerked the reins, a warning to Mike to exercise caution. The mare snorted scornfully, and started down the incline at a fast pace. Midway she slipped and cried out. Tad pulled her to an abrupt stop, and after a brief pause they went on again, but this time Mike made no attempt to hurry. When they reached the foot of the incline, they found the girl awaiting them.

"All right?" she asked over her shoulder.

"Sure," Tad answered.

"Then come on," she said and rode off again.

Tad frowned; he didn't like being hurried about, particularly by a girl. But he quickly forgot his resentment. The girl was uncommonly pretty. He spurred Mike, sent her bounding ahead. Minutes later they overtook the girl, ranged themselves alongside. Together they rode swiftly and steadily southward.

CHAPTER TWO

The Walker spread was neither an elaborate affair nor a choice location.

The layout was fairly level, with a few acres under cultivation and with others in process of being planted. The acreage itself was triangular in shape, with the widest part occupied by the house, a barn, and two shacks that were evidently a storehouse and a workshop or tool shed. The land narrowed sharply as it spread away; there were trees along the southern border, and high, uneven, boulder-dotted land forming the northern limits. As the spread narrowed, the trees seemed to thicken, while the boulders became bigger and more numerous. The overall and immediate impression created was that of a huge pincers with nature's hand about to close the pincers and squeeze the very life out of the homestead. Tad's keen eyes ranged over the place, returning presently to the house itself: It was an odd-looking affair; actually it had long since ceased to be a single building. After studying it briefly, Tad decided that it had doubtless started life as a two room cottage and that wings had been added to it at what he judged had been a definitely steady pace. Wherever it was possible, extra rooms had been added and each room took the form of a separate structure that appeared to have been built and then backed into whatever vacant wall space there was left in the original structure, so that now the cottage looked like a body and the new wings like branches or arms and legs. The newest additions, and Tad spotted them without any great effort, sported the freshest looking paint. The main house, he noted, had once been white, time and the elements and probably a not-too-good paint had faded it gray.

There was a barn some fifty feet from the house. It showed where repairs had been made to make the building serviceable. Once there had been an overall paint job of red done on it; the repair boards were untouched and gleamed in their original and virginal natural coloring. There was no corral; neither was there a bunkhouse. Tad was a bit sorry that the Walkers hadn't seen the need for them; they would have made him feel more at home. Of course he wasn't quite certain just what they would have done with either the corral or the bunkhouse; still, he argued, a corral and a bunkhouse, even if they were empty, did things for a place, and this place appeared to be in need of all the help it could get.

The ride southward hadn't been particularly long. At least it hadn't seemed overly long to Tad. True, there had been little conversation, but that had been due largely to the swift pace the girl had set. She had seemed deeply thoughtful, too, and Tad, eyeing her with approval, had refused to intrude upon her thoughts. Her preoccupation gave him an excellent opportunity to study her without being detected, and he found himself quite pleased with the subject matter she presented. They had pulled up midway between the barn and the house, idled there for a minute or two while he looked the place over. The barn took the least time. He glanced at it and promptly forgot about it. Truthfully, he forgot about her too—that is for that very brief minute or two pause. When she swung herself out of the saddle, he was jerked back to reality. She looked up at him patiently, smiled a bit.

"We-ll," she said presently. "This is it. This is home."

He eased himself, kicked his long legs free of the stirrups.

"Looks all right to me," he observed with masculine finality.

She nodded somewhat absently.

"O-h," she said as an afterthought. "What's your name?"

"It's Tad," he answered. "Tad Cole."

"C-o-l-e?"

"Uh-huh," he said gravely. "My right name's Thaddeus on'y I never tell 'nybody. Tad's bad enough but anything is better'n Thaddeus."

She smiled understandingly, a warm, crinkly, friendly smile that parted her lips and revealed white, even teeth framed in as pleasant and interesting a face as he had ever seen.

"Being named Thaddeus didn't make life at school any too easy for you, did it?"

"Nope," he said. She liked the way his blue eyes twinkled when he smiled. "I had to take on practic'lly every kid in the county b'fore I found out about Tad. I've never answered to anything else since then."

"How did you come to Thaddeus?"

"O-h," he said, "Ma hung it on me. Y'see, her on'y brother was an actor and Ma allus kinda looked up t' him. Anyway, the best part he ever played was a character named Thaddeus. When I was born and it came t' picking out a name f'r me, things kinda narrowed down to Felix, my uncle's real name, and this blamed Thaddeus."

"And Thaddeus won out."

"It wasn't even a fight," he said disgustedly. "It was a walkaway for Thaddeus."

"I wonder," she mused, "if you'd been any happier as Felix?"

"Six o' one, half a dozen o' the other."

"Y-es, I suppose that's so. Still, a name's only a name, and nothing more."

"Maybe," he said, but she knew he was unconvinced. "What's your name?"

"Walker," she said simply.

"You don't say!" he said. There was feigned surprise in his voice. "From what I've seen and heard, there must be more'n just one Walker around here. How do folks tell you Walkers apart?"

She blushed prettily; it began at her neck and throat and ranged upward over her face and surged under the blonde hair that peeked out from under the red ribbon, and finally lost itself in the ribbon's brighter red.

"I'm sorry," she said. "I meant to say Eve Walker."

"H-m," he said. "No actors in your fam'ly, huh?"

"Only farmers."

"Eve," he repeated and he looked skyward for a moment. "Eve."

"Don't you—like it?"

"O-h, sure! And it fits you, too."

"Thank you," she said. She watched as he swung himself off Mike's back. He slung the reins over Mike's head, disregarded the mare when she nudged him with her head. "Tad."

"Huh? What'd you say, Eve?"

"I know I should have said this sooner, anyway we're all terribly grateful to you."

"Forget it."

"She looked up at him for a moment.

"We'd better go in now," she said.

"Wait a minute," he said hastily. "Y'mean we gotta go inside so's the rest o' your folks c'n tell me what a hero I am?"

"They'd be strange people if they didn't say something, wouldn't they?"

"Yeah, I suppose so," he replied slowly. "Look, Eve, you tell 'em you've said it f'r all 'o them, will you? Then some day when I come by again, I'll stop and meet 'em all. All right?"

"Yes, of course," she said.

She turned on her heel and strode off.

"Damnation," he muttered.

He wheeled and ran after her, reached the back door a step ahead of her, twisted the knob, opened the door and held it wide, then mumbling something to himself, followed her inside. The door slammed against him and he glared at it over his shoulder.

"Look, Eve," he began. Suddenly he was aware of other faces, strange faces and strange people—a white-haired man, a couple of husky young men who were looking at him with more than just casual interest. He flushed, took off his hat.

"Pa," he heard Eve say, and the white-haired man arose from his chair at the kitchen table. "This is Tad Cole."

The elder Walker held out his hand. Tad hastily shifted his hat to his left hand, gripped Walker's hand with his right hand, shook it gravely.

"Tad doesn't like being fussed over," Eve went on. She took him by the arm, led him around the table. "This is my brother, Dan."

A hand that was like a vise gripped Tad's.

"Glad to know you," Dan said simply.

"Tad, this is Walt," Eve said, and another Walker thrust out his hand, smiled at Tad, shook hands with him and stepped back. There was still another Walker, a youngster of about nineteen who grinned at him.

"Hi," he said simply but adequately.

"That's Eddie," Eve said. "One of the twins."

"Hi," Tad acknowledged.

He wondered why young Abel Walker—Curly, Cahill had called him—wasn't there too.

"Allie," Eve said, and another young man who bore no resemblance at all to the others came forward. "Tad, this is Allen Clark. We call him Allie."

Clark shook hands with Tad, turned without a word and moved away. A moment later he left the room. No one seemed to notice it—at least, no one paid any attention to his leaving. There was a light step and when Tad looked up there was a girl standing in the connecting doorway between the kitchen and what he assumed was the parlor. She was taller than Eve, and Tad told himself begrudgingly, she was even prettier.

"Hello," she said brightly and smiled at him.

"Tad," Eve said. "This is my sister, Doreen."

Doreen came into the room. She stopped beside Dan, slipped her arm through his. She turned to Tad again, looked at him calmly, appraisingly. Tad's eyes wavered, fell before hers. He grinned a bit nervously, twisted his hat around in his hands. Dan came to his rescue.

"What d'you say we eat?" he asked.

"Supper's ready," Doreen answered. "One of you boys show Tad where he can wash up."

Dan hitched up his pants.

"C'mon, Tad," he said.

Tad moved forward to join him so quickly that he collided with Eve, mumbled an apology, circled around her and then trod on Dan's heels in his eagerness to get out of the room.

When supper was over, Dan led Tad out of the house. Walt and Eddie followed, then Allen Clark sauntered out.

"Eddie," Dan said over his shoulder. "Get Tad's horse, and saddle up a couple for Walt and me."

"Yeah, sure," the boy answered. He stepped past them, strode briskly away toward the barn.

"Walt and me'll ride a ways with you," Dan said to Tad.

"No need for that," Tad said quickly.

The back door opened and Pa Walker emerged. He handed Dan a rifle, handed one to Walt, too. There was a clatter of hoofs and Eddie, astride a big white horse and leading Mike and a third horse, rode out of the barn. He pulled up in front of them, slipped to the ground lightly. Mike whinnied softly and Tad, stepping up to her, patted her neck, gripped the reins, caught the saddle horn with his left hand, swung himself up on her back. He wheeled the mare just as Dan and Walt were mounting their horses.

"All right?" Dan called.

Walt and Tad answered in unison.

"Right."

There were no good-byes; in the fading light Pa Walker, Eddie and Allen Clark waved, and Tad acknowledged in like fashion; then, with Dan in the lead and Walt riding alongside of Tad, they clattered away. They loped past the barn, swung eastward. Tad turned briefly and looked back. There was a girl standing in the kitchen doorway. When she waved something white, probably a dish towel, Tad responded. He hoped it was Eve. He settled himself in the saddle, wondering the while when he would see her again.

Tad turned to Walt.

"Wanted to ask b'fore," he said. "Curly—is he all right?"

"O-h, sure," Walt answered. "Course he should've come out to meet you and say somethin', but Doreen said he didn't feel up to it. Seems like all he wanted t' do was sprawl out on his back on his bed and stare up at the ceilin'. After a while, Doreen'll get him to come out and eat somethin'. She knows how t' handle him. He'll be all right by mornin'."

I don't blame him for not wantin' to be bothered by anyone," Tad said. "He sure went through somethin' today."

"He did at that," Walt acknowledged. "And it would've been a heap worse f'r him if you hadn't been there to take over after Eve jumped the gun on us and nearly messed up the hull thing."

"What do you mean?"

"O-h, we had it all planned how we were gonna get Curly away. We were gonna jump the sheriff's office in the middle o' the night and get Curly out."

"I see."

"We figgered we'd have a better chance then than if we tried 'nything in the open."

"There's a lotta credit comin' to Eve anyway. It took plenty o' guts to try what she did."

"Yeah, sure."

"Think they'll come after you folks again?" Tad asked.

"What d'you think?" Walt answered.

"I think you menfolks better sleep with your boots on," Tad said briefly.

"We're plannin' t' do more'n that."

"That so?"

"We're gonna take turns, Dan, Allie and me, standin' guard during the night."

"You'll live longer that way," Tad said grimly.

They reached the woodland and Dan, wheeling ahead of them, waited until they rode up. It was dusk now and great, awing shadows reached out from among the trees. Tad looked backward. The barn loomed up in the enveloping night light, a huge distorted hulk of a structure. One or two lights gleamed in the windows of the house. It seemed far away.

"Which way do I go?" Tad asked, turning again.

"We'll show you," Dan replied.

He clattered away before Tad could stop him, rode in among the trees; Tad and Walt followed. The woodland was silent, hushed; there was an eerie, even ominous stillness among the trees. The men sensed it at once, sat upright, their hands close to their guns; the horses reacted to it, too. Mike whinnied as she went on. Now, far into the wooded section, all light seemed to have turned out behind them. They checked their horses, slowed them to a walk. The grass was thick and it cushioned their hoofbeats. A shadow leaped out from behind a tree and Mike screamed in terror, shied away, collided with Walt's mount. Then in a twinkling other shadows darted out, shadows that moved as only men move.

A voice cried out in the darkness ahead of them. It was Dan's.

A shadow leaped into Mike's path, reached for the mare's bridle; Tad, on the alert, lifted his left foot free of the stirrup, drew his leg back, then he drove it, heel first, into the shadowy figure's face. The man melted away into dark nothingness. The others sprang up, as if out of the very ground, pounced upon them, and a wild melee followed. Tad and Walt, fighting them off, used their guns like clubs, bashing in heads that came close enough to be bashed in. A horseman that was Dan Walker fought his way back to their side, then flank to flank and knee to knee the three struck back. Shadowy figures swarmed forward continually, clutching at bridles and stirrups, legs and arms, and seeking too to reach the men astride their horses, to pull them from their saddles.

It was a strange fight, a weird fight, too, and something new for Tad. There was no gunplay—this was a close-quarter fight with plunging, frightened horses hemmed in a small circle of space, their riders struggling to keep their seats astride them, with tight-lipped grunts and thuds following the landing of each blow. Here and there a dark, indistinguishable figure simply sagged beneath a sweeping, thudding gun butt, tottered away and disappeared into the thick blackness. Dan's rifle, its stock already smashed, was torn out of his hands. He gripped the reins, drove his spurs deep into his mount's flanks. The horse, already terrified, screamed, then plunged away blindly with two men clinging to his bridle and a third hanging on to Dan's left leg. Dan swung his blood-drenched gun aloft, brought it down with a resounding whack on one man's head and the hapless man slipped away limply. The second man abandoned the attack when a spurred heel dug deep into his face. The third man was crushed against a tree.

Dan's sweeping gun butt drove off two of Tad's attackers, his free hand whacked Walt's horse across the rump and the animal cried out, reared up, clearing a path for both Mike and himself. A second stinging slap from Dan's uncompromising hand set Walt's mount bounding away. Mike needed no urging. She simply leaped forward, brushing men aside, trampling some, too, and then the three horses were whirling out of the woodland. Now the frustrated attackers opened fire on them, but it was too late. Given their heads, the frightened horses lurched and plunged and thundered away in that one mad bid for freedom. They tore out of the trees like runaways, whirled and went racing over the ground at a furious gait, their pounding hoofs echoing. It seemed an incredibly scant few minutes later when they were pulling up at the back door. Three rifle-armed figures, then a fourth one, burst out, raced past them; a moment later rifle fire roared.

There was confusion at the kitchen door when Dan and Walt dismounted and rushed into the house in search of rifles. They emerged presently empty-handed. Presently too the rifle fire died out. Pa Walker, Allen Clark, Eddie and Curly came trudging back to report that the raiders had gone. Dan smiled grimly.

"They won't come 'round here again for a long time," he asserted, and Tad and Walt, who were still panting, did not dispute him. Tad looked at him but Dan avoided his eyes and Tad decided that Dan was simply trying to ease the others' fears. The raiders, whoever they were, would return, Tad knew, and he knew that Dan knew it too. "We musta busted pretty nearly every head in Shorthorn," Dan continued. "It's gonna take a long, long time f'r tonight's headaches to wear off. S-ay, you fellers, Tad, Walt—how 'bout something to eat, huh? I'm plumb empty again."

Doreen laughed.

"All right, you wolves," she said. "Sit down. I'll put the coffee on."

They seated themselves at the kitchen table. Eddie and Curly, excited and still breathing hard and noisily, stood around them, eyeing them with boyish admiration, watching their every move, hanging on everything they said.

"Tad," Eve said suddenly and she bent over him and touched his left hand. There was a widening streak of blood on his knuckles. "You're hurt."

Dan bolted out of his chair; he came striding around the table, looked carefully at Tad's hand. He straightened up presently.

"Better let Eve take care of it," he said briefly.

"T'aint more'n a scratch," Tad said quickly.

Dan caught his eye, winked at him.

"A scratch?" he repeated. "Heck, man, that hand's busted wide open. It's gonna take a heap o' tendin' to before you'll be able to use it again. Darned lucky thing f'r you that Eve knows how t' treat it."

He backed away from the table to permit Eve to pass him. She placed a basin of water and vinegar in front of Tad, deftly cut some strips of white cloth, put them on the table, too. She pushed back her sleeves, then she took Tad's hand in hers, slid it into the basin. Tad grimaced.

"It's the vinegar," she said quickly. "It stings a bit as it cleanses."

Dan had seated himself again. He watched for a moment as Eve dried Tad's hand in a towel she had slung over her shoulder, watched her bandage the hand, then he sat back in his chair.

"Looks like you're gonna hafta stay put here f'r a while, Tad," he said. "Eve don't b'lieve in lettin' her patients off the premises till she's satisfied there won't be 'ny relapses. That is, ordinarily. 'Course there was one time when—"

Eve jerked her head up.

"Dan!" she said severely.

"Huh?' Dan asked. "I wasn't gonna say 'nything. I just wanted t' tell Tad about that Wiley feller."

"Tad isn't at all interested in anything concerning Luther Wiley."

Dan shrugged his shoulder.

"All right, if you say so. Only it makes me laugh everytime I think o' what that Wiley feller looked like with the dog hangin on t' the seat o' his pants. And when he fin'lly went home, wearing one o' your old skirts over his pants, that was somethin' to see."

"No one else even tried to help the poor man."

"He didn't come callin' on me," Dan said stoutly. "He was your feller. He was courtin' you, wasn't he?"

"Wait a minute, Dan," Walt said. "Seems t' me that I did somethin' for him. 'Course I couldn't sew up his pants. But I did lay him out here on the table and kinda soothe the spots where the dog nipped 'im."

"I wanted t' do somethin' for 'im," Dan said protestingly.

"Wa-al," Walt demanded, "what stopped you?"

"I couldn't stop laughing," Dan admitted sheepishly.

Eve snatched up the towel, picked up the basin and went out of the room. As she passed her father, who was sitting quietly in a corner of the room, she glanced at him. Their eyes met and a smile passed between them.

CHAPTER THREE

It was dawn when Tad slipped out of the sleeping house and closed the back door quietly behind him, wondering the while why it had been left unlocked. It was a drab, chilly dawn, with a cold mist filming the air, and an offensive-smelling dampness on the ground and above it. The dawn sky was dull and grayish, and the horizon beyond it was draped in shadowy, motionless darkness. A light twinkled briefly in the sky, like a distant candle sputtering in the face of a breeze; a moment later it was gone, snuffed out. But it reappeared shortly, and this time it flamed brighter than before, until the horizon was alight from end to end. The light deepened and the shadowy veil was whisked away. The sky brightened, glowed with a warming radiance. The mist dissolved, and the damp smell vanished as the sweet fragrance of freshly plowed earth filled the air.

Tad looked down at his bandaged hand, eyed it with disgust; he raised it to his nose, sniffed it, made a wry face and hastily put it down.

"Do you always get up this early?" a voice asked and he looked up quickly.

It was Doreen, a bucket of water in her hand, coming down the trampled grass and dirt path from the barn. She stopped in front of him. She was just as pretty in the awakening daylight as she had been the evening before. She was clad in dungarees and jacket and when she turned down her jacket collar he caught a glimpse of a heavy plaid shirt beneath it.

"O-h," he said and touched the brim of his hat. "G'morning."

"Good morning, Tad. Do you always get up so early?"

"Nope," he admitted calmly. "Most o' the time, leastways when I get the chance, I c'n sleep clear around the clock. But this wasn't one o' those times. I kept smellin' vinegar all night long, and finally when I got plumb tired o' turnin' and tossin', I got outta bed, got dressed and came out, hopin' the fresh air might do some good. How come you're up and doin' already?"

She followed his eyes. Her hair was golden rather than blond; it seemed to fascinate him.

"I've been doing some doctoring," she answered. "One of our mares has just foaled a colt."

"O-h," he said again. "I was wonderin' why the back door was open. I didn't expect t' find 'nybody else up, least of all, you."

She smiled. Her eyes never left his face, and it made him feel awkward and embarrassed. Her eyes were clear and wide and as blue as an evening sky. Yet they seemed to be filled will a curious, unexplainable taunting even though there was nothing of a challenging nature in her manner. She shifted the pail to her other hand; finally she set it down on the ground.

"Where do you come from, Tad?" she asked.

"Kansas."

"We're from Missouri."

"Sorry you left there?"

She considered his question for a moment.

"No," she said shortly. "I like the West. Of course it isn't exactly the way I'd hoped it would be, still I'm not at all sorry that we came out here."

"Even though the goin' gets tough every once in a while?"

She smiled quietly.

"We've always been able to take care of ourselves," she said. "Sometimes we need help, just as we did yesterday, but all in all we usually manage to give as good as we get. Will you mind very much if I say, 'thanks a million' for helping Curly out of a tight spot?"

"Will you promise not t' mention it again?"

"I won't," she said, "if you'd rather I didn't."

She held out her right hand. They shook hands gravely. The back door opened and they turned as one. Allen Clark was framed in the doorway.

"Morning, Allie," Doreen called.

"Mornin'," Clark answered. He nodded to Tad. He stepped out, turned and caught the door as it swung past him, closed it, then sauntered forward, and finally stopped a few feet from them. "Hope I didn't interrupt 'nything."

"Silly," Doreen said quickly. She picked up the bucket. "I'll have breakfast ready in a few minutes."

She went into the house.

Tad, his thumbs hooked in his gun belt, and Clark, his hands on his hips, looked at each other. Clark, Tad noted, was heavier than he was, thicker through the shoulders. He was almost as tall as Tad, too. He was a good-looking man, and Tad was certain that he had discovered some resentment in Clark's eyes. Allie's eyes ranged over Tad, lingered for a moment on Tad's low-hanging Colt, then he raised them again to meet Tad's.

"Which way you headed, Cole?" he asked presently.

"O-h, no place in p'rticular," Tad replied. "Had 'n idea I might like t' see what California's like. Now I ain't so sure."

"Hightailin' it?"

"Nope," Tad said curtly. "Are you?"

Clark's lips tightened.

"You got all the markin's of a ranch hand," he said. "How come you took up for a nester?"

"Maybe it was b'cause he was on'y a kid, and it looked t' me like he was up against a cold deck."

Cole smiled disbelievingly.

"You oughta be able t' do better'n that," he said chidingly.

" 'Course," Tad said evenly, "if it was you they were readyin' f'r a hangin', chances are I'da minded my own bus'ness and that woulda been that. But Curly looked like a nice kid, so I just natur'lly had to horn in. Anything else botherin' you this early in the mornin' or are you always so danged ornery lookin' and ornery soundin'?"

"I don't like heroes, mister," he said darkly. "Not even real ones."

"Reckon that's one o' the things that helps make this country a free country," Tad answered. "Every man's entitled t' have his own p'rticular likes and dislikes. But if I were you, Clark, I wouldn't lose 'ny sleep 'bout this hero business. I don't think there's much chance o' anyone ever havin' t' accuse you o' bein' a hero, not even a fake hero."

Clark's lips thinned out again.

"Cole," he began.

"Yeah?" Tad asked tauntingly.

"I'm gonna give you a tip. You c'n take it or leave it."

Tad smiled fleetingly.

"That's big o' you, givin' me my choice. But since it's comin' fr'm you, Clark, I'm so doggoned anxious t' hear what it is, I c'n hardly wait."

"This place ain't big enough f'r both of us. I aim t' stay put here. That clear?"

"Yeah, sure. On'y I aim t' stay put here, too, leastways till I'm good and ready to go, and not b'fore. That clear enough f'r you, or do I hafta draw you some pictures?"

Allie Clark hitched up his pants.

"From now on it's up t' you," he said curtly. "Just see to it that you stay the hell outta my way."

He strode away toward the barn. Tad followed him with his eyes.

"Clark," he called, and Allie stopped and looked back at him over his shoulder, "where'll you be later on?"

"How much later?"

"O-h, say in about 'n hour."

"Out in the fields. Why?"

"O-h, I just had 'n idea that maybe I'd kinda stop by later on and see you," Tad answered casually.

A smile danced over Clark's lips.

"I'll be lookin' for you," he said.

"I'll be there," Tad said.

Clark went on again, disappeared inside the barn. Tad turned slowly, walked toward the house. He looked up, stopped when he saw Doreen standing in the doorway.

"This Clark feller," he said. "How's he fit into things around here?"

"What do you mean?"

"He part o' the family?"

"O-h, no," she said quickly. "He just works for us."

"I see."

"He came with us from Missouri," Doreen went on. "He hasn't any folks."

"One thing more. He and you supposed to …"

"No," she said. "Why did you ask me those things about Allie?"

He grinned at her.

"Reckon that's just a sign of advancin' old age. I'm gettin' more an' more curious all the time. Plumb disgustin' ain't it?"

"Tad," she said.

"Yeah?"

"You aren't a very good liar, are you?"

"Meaning?"

"It wasn't just idle curiosity that prompted those questions about Allie. You asked them for a purpose."

"You're wrong there, Doreen. I asked because I really wanted t' know. That's all there was to it. Honest."

Her eyes probed his face.

"All right," she said finally, "if you say so. Ready for your breakfast?"

"I on'y want some coffee."

"The biscuits are ready. You'll have some, won't you?"

"Just the coffee, thanks."

She turned without another word, and stepped back into the house. Tad followed her inside, dropped his hat into a chair near the door, then he sat down at the table. She brought him a cup of coffee, watched as he drank it. When he had drained the cup, he put it down.

"More?" she asked.

"Nope. That'll hold me."

He climbed to his feet, strode over and picked up his hat, opened the door.

"Where are you going?" Doreen asked.

"O-h, I'm just gonna have a look around."

"But you'll be back, won't you?"

He smiled at her, shifted his holster mechanically. "Sure," he said and went out.

He found Clark sitting on a tree stump in the middle of a plowed field. Allie turned when he heard Tad's crunching boot step, laughed and got to his feet.

"Hi, hero," Allie called.

"Hi, y'self," Tad responded as he came up to him.

Clark laughed again.

"This spot suit you?" he asked.

"Yeah, sure."

Both took off their hats, dropped them on the ground. When Tad unbuttoned and took off his shirt, Allie took off his shirt. Tad unbuckled his gun belt, placed it under his hat. Then without further ado, they simply faced each other and squared off. Allie came in close, drove a hard punch into the body but Tad managed to block it partially with his arm; Allie grunted, came in again but this time Tad side-stepped and drove a long left into Clark's face. Tad followed it up instantly, pumped two more lightning punches into Allie's face. He grinned when blood flecked Clark's face.

Allie plunged in. He landed with both hands, short, powerful blows to the body, but as he stepped back, Tad's long right landed square on Clark's mouth. Allie spat out a tooth, came whirling in, swarmed over Tad, battered him savagely about the body. Tad, panting and breathing through the mouth, fought his way out of it. Clark was breathing hard, and he lowered his hands for a moment. This time it was Tad who plunged into the attack. Clark fought back manfully, driving his big fists into Tad's body while Tad's fists beat a crunching tattoo on Allie's face.

It was a strange fight, almost like the fight in the woods the previous night. Neither man uttered a word; there was no sound save the thud of landing blows, a grunt when the blows landed squarely, the sound of booted feet moving about on the rough, upturned earth. A powerful punch that burst through Tad's guard and landed square in the pit of his stomach brought a gasp from Tad and dropped him on his hands and knees. Allie stood close by, waiting, his big hands raised and poised.

"Got enough?" he asked.

Tad raised his head and grinned up at him.

"Nope," he replied.

He forced himself up presently, backed away from Allie's menacing fists, held him off with a long, darting left. When he felt stronger, he plunged in recklessly, caught Allie off balance with a glancing right to the jaw and Clark went over backwards, sprawled out on the turf on the seat of his pants.

"How you doin'?" Tad asked with a grin.

"That was 'n accident," Allie answered. "You couldn't do that again in a million years."

"The hell I couldn't!"

Clark scrambled to his feet, started forward only to run into a long left that collided solidly with his left eye. He cursed aloud, plunged in again, swinging wildly and desperately. Now it was

Tad's opportunity and he seized it—or rather his longer legs and longer reach seized it for him. He whirled in and around Clark, side-stepping nimbly, peppered him with punches, took full advantage of the fact that Allie's left eye was tightly closed. He weaved this way and that, drove his punches first to the head and face, then concentrating on Clark's body, battered him about the body with wrist-deep blows. Slowly Allie gave ground, but it afforded him no respite. Tad, sensing victory, threw all caution to the winds. He swarmed over Clark, hammered him with both hands. Allie grunted and winced as Tad's fists landed. He was winded and tired. He staggered under the impact of a barrage of punches, lost all sense of direction when a fist thudded against his right eye and closed it. Tad checked himself.

"Got enough?" he demanded, pantingly.

"Nope," Clark answered through battered teeth and lips. "Come on."

A long, swinging right that landed on the side of Allie's head staggered him again; a second punch that grazed his jaw turned him around on unsteady, wobbling legs. A third blow that carried the full weight of Tad's supple body behind it landed squarely on Clark's jaw, and Allie crashed over sideways, landed on his shoulder, and toppled over on his face in a limp heap. Tad bent over him.

"Hey," he said. "You all right?"

There was no response from Clark.

Tad straightened up. He sauntered over to the tree stump and seated himself on it; minutes later when he felt stronger and equal to movement, he arose and picked up his shirt, mopped his face with the shirttail, then he donned the shirt, buttoned it up. He buckled on his gun belt, put on his hat, and looked over at Clark. Allie was sitting up. His face was battered and bloodied.

"You all right?" Tad asked.

Clark did not answer. Instead, he got to his feet. He hitched up his pants, then he lurched over to where he had dropped his hat and shirt; he bent down, picked up the shirt, managed some-how to get it on, buttoned it up. Tad turned away, plodded off in the direction of the house. As he came abreast of the barn some fifteen minutes later, Dan Walker came out of it, spied Tad and waved to him.

"Hi," Dan called.

"Mornin'," Tad responded.

Dan waited until Tad came up to him. He looked at Tad for a moment, whistled softly.

"Where've you been?" he asked. "You look kinda chewed up."

Tad grinned at him.

"Tangled with a bear," he answered.

"Ain't heard o' any bears 'round these parts," Dan said. "Sure this wasn't a two-legged one?"

"Come t' think of it, he was two-legged."

"What's he look like now?"

"O-h, he's still two-legged. But his face don't look any better'n mine does, and both o' his eyes are closed up f'r the season. Seems t' me too he lost a tooth, or mebbe a couple o' teeth. He looked like he'd had a good goin' over but outside o' that, he'll be as good as new in a couple o' days."

"What was it all about?"

"Just a diff'rence of opinion."

"Nuthin' more personal than that?"

"Nope."

"Got some blood over your face," Dan said, pointing to it. There's a bucket of water standin' just inside the barn door, and if you look around, you'll find a towel hangin' close by."

"Swell."

"Got another shirt?"

"Got a couple o' th'm in my saddle bag."

"Might be a good idea t' change the one you're wearin'. It's kinda bloody and messy."

"Wiped my face with it."

"I c'n see that. Where'd you leave the bear?"

"O-h, out in the fields."

"I'd better go have a look at 'im. You clean up meanwhile. I'll see you when I get back."

They parted. Dan strode off to see the 'bear," while Tad, unbuttoning his shirt again, trudged into the barn.

CHAPTER FOUR

It had been early evening when Tad guided Mike away from the Walker place; it was just about nine o'clock when they pulled up beside the signpost at the entrance to Shorthorn. Earlier there had been a bright moon overhead, and Tad had eyed it with misgivings; now the moon seemed to have disappeared. There was a billowing cloud bank in the sky and he decided that the moon had probably taken refuge behind it. He voiced a hope that the cooperative moon wouldn't hurry to return on his account. He had wanted a dark night for his visit to Shorthorn and now he agreed it was as dark as night as any he had ever known.

In the encompassing darkness the shuttered town looked ghostly. There were two establishments still open, and Tad, viewing them from a distance that rendered positive identification a virtual impossibility, simply decided they were saloons and accepted his own opinion as final. Doubtless he felt secure in that belief because he knew from experience that saloons were always the last to close in any town. Yellow lamplight that gleamed in their windows and stood out so boldly against the totally black surroundings gave the street scene an eerie touch.

Mike disliked darkness, and after what she considered sufficient idling, she whinnied softly; when that failed to move Tad, or arouse him from his motionless silence, she pawed the ground with a show of impatience. Tad jerked the reins sharply, and Mike, who should have known better than to attempt to hurry him into anything, realized in the same moment that she had done the wrong thing. Instantly she subsided. Of course she still nurtured the hope that presently he would be satisfied with having viewed Shorthorn from a distance rather than tempt the fates by entering the shadowy and forbidding-looking town, and that then he would be content to turn around and go back to the Walker place. The barn there was warm and comfortable. Of course there was another reason for Mike's eagerness to get back there, an even more important reason, and that was a handsome gelding that answered to the name of Hal. Mike had attracted his attention, and a shy, sidelong glance at him had caused her heart to turn a handspring. Normally, Mike would have adopted a standoffish attitude so as not to create the impression in Hal's mind that she was a forward female; now it was every mare for herself and all conventions pushed aside because there were two other mares in the Walker barn, two totally unladylike and brazen things who weren't at all interested in or concerned with what others thought of them as long as Hal didn't dislike them. Geldings, Mike told herself, particularly handsome ones, weren't any different from men where forward females were concerned. There was, therefore, no telling just what she would find when she returned there and, womanlike, the thought of those two mares and Hal, alone and unattended, disturbed her. She raised her head, wanted to whinny again in a plea to him to retrace their steps, but she thought better of it and kept her emotions in check. She hoped Hal would be strong. There was nothing she could do at the moment to help him.

Somewhere along the street someone was playing a piano. Presently too, a man with a thick, raspy voice began to sing. Tad frowned as he listened. Even Mike, despite her woes, voiced her opinion of it, a nasally snort that filled with disapproval. The singing was short-lived for a sudden outburst of laughter drowned out the singer. A man staggered out of one of the saloons. Tad watched him, saw him pursue a rather erratic course down the street, saw him turn into a darkened doorway and disappear from sight.

A bit farther down the street, a couple of horses were tied up at a hitching rail. They began to tire of their idleness; they milled about, trampled one another, but after a minute's spirited but aimless pushing and shoving and crowding one another, they abandoned it and quieted down again.

Tad finally wheeled Mike, guided her away from the street, sent her trotting along the back yards until they came to an alley that led to the street. He dismounted, led Mike into the alley, left her with a whispered warning to be quiet, then he went on to the very end of the alley and peered out. There was no one about, and he frowned, although he admitted quite freely that he had no right to expect Cahill to know he was there waiting to see him. But Tad Cole was a lucky young man. As a matter of fact, he was unusually lucky, and perhaps that was why the things he hoped for actually came to pass. It was barely a minute after when a stocky figure emerged from a saloon almost directly across the street, crossed over, and came plodding along in the direction of the alley. It was Cahill, as luck would have it. Tad eyed him, recognized him at once, and grinned broadly.

"There he is, doggone 'im," he muttered gleefully. "That's Shorty, awright."

He wanted to yell out but wisely controlled himself. He knew all too well that it wouldn't do for him to arouse the citizenry. Life, he observed sagely, could be awf'lly short, and he had no desire to remove himself from among the living. Instead, he watched Cahill approach; the man was thirty feet away, twenty, then fifteen, then ten, and Tad quickly pulled back into the darkness and flattened out against a wall, listening intently. When Cahill's footsteps welled, indicating he was almost within reach of the alley, Tad inched his way forward; when the stock figure trudged past, Tad leaped out, clapped a big hand over Cahill's mouth, pinned the man's arms to his sides with his free arm. Cahill struggled manfully.

When he kicked Tad in his shins, Tad winced.

"Doggone it, Shorty," he hissed in Cahill's ear. "Quit it! It's me!"

Cahill evidently recognized his captor's voice even though the supposedly reassuring "It's me" failed to soothe his ruffled feelings and person; at any rate he stopped struggling and permitted Tad to pull him into the protective shadows of the ally. But once within it, he whirled upon Tad wrathfully.

"Blast you!" he hissed back at Tad. "What d'you mean by waylaying me? I ought to set the law on you. I think I will just to teach you a lesson you so richly deserve."

He started out of the alley only to have Tad lunge forward, grab him by the seat of his pants, and pull him back.

"Look, Shorty," Tad warned him. "If you're gonna act up, I'm gonna hafta wallop you one."

"We'll," Cahill said and he chuckled. "How are you, you young rascal?"

"O-h, I'm still able t' sit up and take nourishment. How are you doin'?"

"All right. Now what's this all about?"

"Just wanted t' see you an' mebbe ask you some questions."

"Ask away. And incidentally, where've you been since you left here so hurriedly? With those homesteaders?"

"Uh-huh."

"I thought so. Before I forget this, I owe you a drink."

"Y'do? How come?"

Cahill chuckled again.

"For the delightful wallop you handed our very noble and very righteous Mister Ben Priddy. When I saw the gentleman last, his eye was the nearest thing to a sunset that I've ever seen. I don't believe I've ever looked at anything with a greater sense of delight."

"Who's this Ben Priddy?"

"I forget you hadn't met Priddy formally. Ben Priddy, my boy, is the dirty so-and-so whose lying testimony convicted and nearly caused Curly Walker to join his ancestors ahead of time."

"O-h, yeah?"

"Yes. Priddy was one of those who tried to grab you after Curly effected his getaway. You walloped Priddy beautifully. Thank you, my boy, for doing what I've wanted to do to him ever since the first time I laid eyes on him."

"This Priddy polecat, where's his spread?"

"Where?" Cahill echoed in surprise. "Y'mean you don't know?"

"Look, Shorty...."

"I'm sorry. Priddy's place is south of the Walkers'."

"I see."

Cahill looked at him, waited for a moment, as though he expected Tad to explain what he saw; after a bit, Cahill decided there was no explanation or comment forthcoming.

"I understand you entertained some callers last night," he said.

"Huh? O-h, year! Think they'll come see us again after the way we treated them?"

"But definitely! The skulls you and the Walkers bashed in belong to some of Shorthorn's most illustrious citizens. You don't suppose they intend to forgive and forget what happened to them, do you? Perish the thought, my boy."

"I was on'y wonderin', that's all."

"Then you needn't wonder any longer," Cahill said quickly. "Incidentally, I overheard a very reliable source say tonight that Mister Priddy has suddenly decided he needs and wants the Walker place, so all in all I have an idea that you and your new-found friends are in for a charmingly busy season."

"We c'n handle it," Tad cried. "There's somethin' more important puzzlin' me."

"Y-es?"

"The Hassetts have 'nything worth stealing?"

"I take it you mean worldly goods. If you do, rumor has it that they struck gold, and quite a lot of it, too. Enough to make robbery the primary motive for their murders. Does that help you any?"

"Some. Where's it now?"

"The gold? That, my boy, is what everyone is asking."

"D'you think Priddy got it?"

"No, I don't. And confidentially, I understand he could use a lot of gold to very good advantage."

"Who couldn't?" Tad retorted. "Priddy owe so much?"

"The bank holds a lot of his paper," Cahill explained.

"O-h. But if he didn't get it, who do'you suppose did?"

"A-h, now there's a question! Frankly, and even though I haven't any reason for thinking this, it's my opinion, or hunch if you like, that the Hasset gold is still where the late departed and unlamented brothers cached it."

"If that's so then your Mister Priddy must figger that Curly knows where it is."

"I think Priddy does believe that."

"Then he won't let up on the Walkers till he gets his hands on Curly again and forces him t' tell."

"Exactly."

Tad was thoughtfully silent for a moment.

"S-ay," he said finally. "Where c'n I get hold o' you if I want you?"

"I live in the shack behind Crosby's general store."

"Where's that? I mean Crosby's?"

"Down the street, third store from the corner."

"I'll remember it. Mind if I ask you somethin' else, somethin' personal?"

Cahill drew a deep breath.

"What's your angle? What d'you do around here? You aren't a cowman. You don't act like one, and you sure don't talk like one."

"O-h, I just live here. That's all."

"That's all, huh?"

"Yes."

Tad hitched up his pants.

"You oughta know," he said. "I'd better get goin'. But I'll prob'bly be seein' you again one o' these nights."

"I shall look forward to it."

Tad grunted, turned on his heel and trudged down the length of the alley. A minute later Cahill heard him ride out. He turned slowly, stopped almost immediately.

"Confound it," he muttered. "That's the second time I forgot to ask him his name."

The moon reappeared shortly before Tad reached the Walker place. Mike's spirits seemed to perk up in the brighter light; a second reason was the fact that they were now in sight of the barn. Mike whinnied once or twice, even quickened her pace of her own accord. Tad made no attempt to restrain her. They loped around to the front of the barn, pulled up at the door. A slim figure was standing in the doorway.

"H'llo," Tad called.

"Hello," came the answer and he was surprised to hear Eve's voice.

He dismounted, looped the ends of the reins around the saddle horn.

"G'wan inside," he said and Mike jogged into the barn. Tad stopped in front of Eve. He pushed his hat up from his eyes. "Gettin' some fresh air for y'self?"

"I'm waiting for my brother," she answered.

"Curly?"

"Yes."

There was a brief, awkward silence.

"Where'd he go?" he asked finally. "Maybe I could kinda ride out t' meet him?"

She considered for a moment, then shook her head.

"No," she said.

He shrugged his shoulder.

"Whatever you say," he said. "I'd s'ggest that we both go, just f'r a ride, y'know, on'y it ain't exactly safe."

She looked at him quickly, anxiously.

"You think they're still looking for him?"

"My guess ain't 'ny better 'n yours. All I know is that they were here last night."

He glanced toward the house. He couldn't tell much from the light in the kitchen.

"How about the boys?" he asked. "Dan and Walt—they still up?"

"They were half an hour ago. But I'd rather they didn't know."

"Look," he said. "I'll ride out a ways, circle around and work my way back here. Maybe I'll run into 'im."

"It's awf'lly sweet of you, Tad, to bother."

He grinned at her.

"But it's no go," he said, " 'less you turn in. No point in both of us losin' sleep over the same thing, y'know."

"No," she said determinedly. "I'll wait right here till you get back."

"We-ll …."

"Please."

He turned, stepped into the doorway.

"Mike," he called again, this time a bit sharper.

The mare answered. Eve heard her. It sounded like a protest. Tad strode into the barn. He reappeared a moment later, leading Mike by the bridle, led her outside.

"Mike and that gelding o' yours've got a crush on each other," Tad said with a grin. "You oughta see the look they gave me."

He swung himself up astride Mike's back.

"Please be careful," Eve said.

"I'm always careful," Tad said over his shoulder as he rode away.

They swept wide of the house, loped out onto the open range. It was a beautiful night; the air was crisp and sweet, and Tad breathed in deeply. He settled himself in the saddle.

"That danged kid," he muttered to himself. "Wonder where'n hell he went to?"

He frowned darkly, pulled his hat down a bit.

"What would a kid like him be doin' out this late at night?" he asked himself. "b'sides, he knows just as well as I do that Priddy and the law are out gunnin' f'r 'im, so you'd think he'd have sense enough t' stay put, leastways till things quiet down some."

He shifted himself in the saddle, eased himself a little.

"But bein' that he's still on'y a kid," he observed, "expectin' him t' have sense is expectin' a lot."

He nudged Mike with his knees and the mare, resigned to her unhappy fate, broke in a brisk canter. They rode westward for half a mile, halted briefly, then they swung northward, pulled up for a minute; Tad's eyes probed the moonlit range, but there was nothing to be seen. He mumbled something under his breath. The word "damn" was audible and understandable above the other words. They turned eastward presently. The night breeze droned past them, whipped through the range grass, raced away southward. Then they were within sight of the woods. Mike slackened her pace, hesitated as though she were pleading with Tad not to attempt to ride through the shadow-shrouded trees. Tad frowned again, tightened his grip on the reins. Mechanically his right hand dropped, closed around the butt of his Colt.

"Go on," he said curtly and they rode into the woods.

A swinging branch from a thick-trunked tree slashed Mike and she screamed, shied away from it in fright. Then shadowy figures that seemed to rise up from the ground leaped upon them, tore Tad's gun out of his hand, dragged him out of the saddle, bore him to the ground. Strong hands gripped his wrists and arms. He lashed out blindly with his feet. A man cursed and a fist struck him squarely in the face. He kicked again; his booted foot drove deep into a man's stomach and the man cried out. Tad wrenched himself away, plunged away blindly. He stumbled over a half-buried rock, fell on his hands and knees. He scrambled to his feet, turned and ran into a swarm of shadowy figures. His fits cleared a path for him, then a man hurled himself upon Tad's back and they went down in a swirling tangle of arms and legs. A gun butt flashed upward, downward, thudded on his bared head and he grunted, sagged, and toppled over in an unconscious heap.

CHAPTER FIVE

M iles away from the triangular-shaped spread that formed the Walker layout, atop a flat rise that looked down upon the Priddy ranch, Curly Walker was crouched behind a burnt-out tree stump. There was a liberal sprinkling of stumps on the rise which jutted out from the range itself like a shelf; scattered about were a couple of lopsided boulders, startlingly white in the moonlight, their sun-bleached faces gleaming with an eye-arresting brightness. Curly noticed it, and he felt uneasy about it, for in their almost human faces he fancied he could see completely human faces, the faces of imaginary possemen whom he was momentarily expecting to find rising up all around him. He was never without that fear and he found himself straining whenever he heard or thought he heard a strange sound. Then, too, there was that never-to-be forgotten scene in the courtroom, and the sense of being at death's door and then being dragged back.... He couldn't crowd them out of his thoughts. He wondered how it would all come out, wondered if he would ever again feel free and safe.

He studied the ranchhouse below him. It was a big, sprawling affair, much bigger than his own. There was the bunkhouse beyond it, a squat, low structure. He had heard that Priddy's outfit was the biggest in the country, that some thirty punchers rode the Priddy fences and herd. The corral was somewhere close by the bunkhouse; even though he couldn't see it from where he was crouched, he could hear horses moving and milling about. His eyes went back to the ranchhouse. There was a light in the kitchen, and a light, a bit softer than the garishly yellow light in the kitchen, in a room on the upper floor. As he watched, the window in the second floor room was raised; a pair of sturdy arms did the raising. His pulse quickened and for the moment he forgot his fears. The head and shoulders of a slim, girlish figure appeared in the window. His lips moved.

"Lila," he whispered.

It was strange, his being there. He had seen her just once, and he had never forgotten her. He knew he would never forget her. He had been riding past a Priddy fence when she appeared. He stopped, looked at her and she had looked at him.

"H'llo," he recalled that he had said.

She was slim and straight with gentle brown eyes framed in a milky skinned oval face. Her hair was brown too, and she wore it in braids wound around her head.

"H'llo," he had said a second time.

"Hello," she answered.

She looked at him interestedly, calmly but not appraisingly, and he laughed awkwardly.

"S'matter?" he asked. "Do I look funny?"

"Oh, no," she answered quickly. "I think you're nice. I'm Lila. Lila Priddy. What's your name?"

So she was Priddy's daughter. Priddy, who was so sternfaced and cold-eyed, and this was his daughter.

"I'm Curly Walker," he said quietly.

"Walker?" she repeated. "O-h you're one of those awful homesteaders!"

He remembered how he had stiffened, how he'd wheeled his horse, how she'd run after him along the fence.

"Please!" she called. "Please wait!"

He pulled up, turned slowly in the saddle and looked down at her.

"I'm sorry," she said meeting his eyes. "I'm terribly sorry."

All the anger and resentment that had flared up within him vanished in that instant and he remembered that he had smiled again.

"Aw, forget it," he had said.

He had dismounted; they had stood, with the fence between them, and talked. Then it was time for her to go.

"Do you come this way often?" she asked.

"That d'pends," he replied.

"On what?" she pressed.

"O-h, on whether I want to or not," he said with a casual air.

She was silent then.

"How 'bout you?" he asked.

"I like to walk through the fields," she answered.

"And do you always walk up this way?"

She tossed her head.

"Whenever I feel like it," she said.

He grinned at her boyishly and her eyes faltered for a moment.

"Think you're gonna feel like it t'morrow?" he asked.

"Tomorrow I'm going into town with my mother."

"What about the next day?"

"Emma Lane's coming over for the day."

He didn't bother to ask her who Emma was; she might be big or little, slim or fat, and he felt no interest in her.

"We-ll how about the day after that?" he asked.

"Will you ride this way then?" she countered.

He nodded gravely. She raised her head again and their eyes met.

"Well?" he asked.

"Thursday," she said.

"Swell."

He went back to his horse, climbed into the saddle, wheeled and rode away. He looked back once over his shoulder; she was still standing at the fence. He whipped off his hat, waved it and she waved her hand in answer. That was the last he had seen of her.

But he hadn't forgotten her for he knew he would never be able to do that. In jail, in the courtroom, when he was awake, even when he was asleep, her face always appeared in his mind's eye. She would smile at him, and her lips would move, and he would strain to catch what she was saying. Now he was crouching behind a protecting tree stump, hoping to catch even the barest glimpse of her. The bunkhouse door slammed and his eyes shifted to it. When they went back, she was gone and the light in her room was turned out. He sighed deeply, turned and crept back to the thicket in which he had tethered his horse. Minutes later he reappeared, leading the animal by the bridle. Quickly he vaulted into the saddle, guided his horse away, rode off into the silver night.

Tad groaned. A heavy booted foot crashed against his ribs.

"Get on your feet!" a cold voice commanded.

Tad opened his eyes. He blinked when a lighted match was suddenly thrust into his face. When it flared up, he pulled back out of range. He caught a glimpse of grim hostile faces above him.

"It's him awright, boss," a man said.

Another man—Tad couldn't quite see him—snorted.

"I knew it wasn't that punk kid right off," he said gruffly. "No homesteader's got guts enough t' fight back when he's hit."

A third man pushed his way into the circle of men surrounding Tad. He dropped to one knee beside Tad. He was middle-aged, sharp-faced and his steely eyes burned into Tad's.

"You," he said curtly. "What's your name?"

"Cole."

"Is it yours or someb'y else's?"

"Mine."

"Where d'you come fr'm?"

"Kansas."

"What do they want you back there fore?"

Tad did not answer.

"Didn't expect you t' answer that one," the man said coldly. "Wouldn'ta b'lieved you anyway. Now listen t' me, an' r'member that Ben Priddy don't talk just t' heard the sound o' his voice. I'm givin' you till t'morrow t' get outta here. After that, an' if you're still around here, my boys are gonna go huntin' for you. An' every time they catch up with you, they're gonna give you the damnedest beatin' anyone ever got. That clear?"

Tad held his tongue. Silence on his part, he decided, was his safest course.

"Where's young Walker?" Priddy demanded.

"Dunno."

The match died out and it was tossed aside. Another was struck; it flamed into light.

"Don't gimme that," Priddy snapped. "Where is he?"

"Home, I s'ppose."

"He is like hell," Priddy said through his teeth, "and you know it. One o' my boys saw him ride away."

"An' if my horse hadn'ta pulled up lame," a man said somewhere in the circle around Tad, "I'da caught up with him an' that woulda been that."

"Where'd he go?" Priddy demanded.

Tad forgot the throbbing in his head for a moment, and shook it negatively. He regretted his forgetfulness almost immediately for the throbbing increased, pounded in his ears, too.

"You're a liar," Priddy said heatedly.

"Boss," a man said behind the rancher, "lemme go t' work on him f'r that kick he gave me in the belly."

Tad smiled inwardly. There was a sense of satisfaction in the knowledge that he had managed to inflict some damage or punishment upon them. Priddy got to his feet.

"Awright," he said, turning to his men. "Let's get goin'. As f'r you, Cole, r'member what I told you. You're gettin' off easy this time. You won't the next time because there won't be another time."

He hitched up his pants, turned on his heel and trudged off. His men followed at his heels. After their footsteps had died away, Tad forced himself up on his knees. He huddled there for a minute or two husbanding his strength. There was a stirring just beyond him and he heard a faint whinny, then Mike was at his side, nudging him with her head.

Tad gripped the saddle with both hands, dragged himself up to his feet. He fell against Mike, rested there briefly, then, with an effort that cost him his last ounce of strength, managed to get his foot into the stirrup. How he ever succeeded in mounting her, he never knew, but presently he was settled in the saddle and Mike was moving forward through the trees. It was minutes later when they emerged into the open, some ten minutes after that when they stopped in front of the barn. Eve came bounding forward to meet them. Tad looked down at her, managed a grin.

"Hello," he said. "I'm back again."

He started to dismount, slipped, made a frantic lunge for the saddle, gripped it with both hands and saved himself from a bad fall.

"Tad," he heard Eve say, "you're hurt!"

"Got a wallop on the head," he answered with an awkward laugh. "Outside o' that I'm almost as good as ever."

Then he realized that her arm was around him, and that she was helping him stand upright. He looked at her, smiled at her reassuringly.

"Thanks," he said. "I'm awright now."

"Sure?"

" 'Course," he said but he did not remove her arm. "Say, did Curly get back?"

"Yes, some time ago."

"Why, the sun-uva-gun! Where'd he say he was, huh?"

"He wouldn't say," Eve answered. "Come on now. We're going into the house. I'm going to have a look at your head."

"Gotta take care o' Mike first," he said.

"Mike," she said firmly, "can wait till you've been attended to."

"You're the boss," he said lightly. "Only there's one thing you've gotta promise me b'fore we go in."

"What's that?"

"No vinegar," he said with grim determination.

It was about two o'clock the next morning when Tad slipped out of the house. Carefully he closed the door behind him. He glanced skyward and frowned; the moon was at its very brightest. He started off toward the barn, stopped as though he had suddenly remembered something he should have done, and hadn't. He put his hand to his head; the bandage that Eve had wound around the lumpy cut on his head was in the house, probably on his bed. Well, it was certain he couldn't go back for it now. He'd have the luck to trip over something and wake the whole household, and then someone, Eve, of course, would have something to say about people who were forever looking for trouble when there was so much of it so close at hand that one had difficulty avoiding it. He'd have to take a chance on getting back to the house before she got up. Fortunately, Doreen was the early riser, so perhaps Eve would never know about the bandage. Anyway, the throbbing in his head had eased up, and so had the pounding that had bothered his ears earlier.

He strode off again. He was near the barn when a husky figure with a rifle in his hands stepped out. It was Walt on watch. Walt looked at him curiously.

"S'matter?" he asked. "What are you doin' up?"

Tad grinned at him.

"O-h, just wanted t' get some fresh air," he answered casually.

"You coulda stuck your head outta your window an' then you'da got your fill of it," Walt observed.

"Yeah, I suppose so."

Tad stepped into the barn, and Walt eyed him again, questioningly.

"Think I'll saddle up an' go f'r a little ride," Tad said, still attempting to be casual.

"F'r a ride?" Walt echoed. "At two o'clock in the mornin'? You gone loco?"

Tad laughed, caught up his saddle and carried it over to Mike's side. The mare eyed him, seemed to shake her head sadly, but she offered no protest when Tad slung the saddle up on her back. Walt stood by quietly.

"Wanna watch y'self when you're out," he cautioned finally. "No tellin' what you're liable t' run into. Which way you aimin' to ride?"

"South, maybe."

"Heck, no!" Walt said quickly. "Priddy's layout is south o' here and there's no tellin' what Priddy'd do t' you if any o' his men caught hold o' you."

"Priddy's place that close?"

"Uh-huh. Ain't more'n 'n hour's ride an' you'd be right smack in his front yard."

"I'll remember that," Tad promised.

He finished saddling Mike, led her outside, climbed up into the saddle and rode away. Walt followed him with his eyes. Just as Tad disappeared into the night, Walt shook his head.

"If that ain't the damnedest thing I ever heard," he muttered. "Gettin' up at two o'clock in the mornin' t' go f'r a ride. He must be goin' loco. Ain't no other way to explain it."

Tad rode eastward for a time, then quickening Mike's pace with an open-handed whack on the rump, he sent her racing away in a southerly direction. He glanced skyward from time to time, eagerly and hopefully, just as he had done earlier, on the ride to

Shorthorn; the fact that luck had favored him then and that the moon had obliged by hiding behind a cloud did not weigh too heavily on his conscience. Luck, he always insisted, never favored the timid—to be lucky one had to force fate to do one's bidding.

"Come on, moon," he urged. "Come on. Be a good fellow an' beat it."

But this time—and for the moment, Tad was very much annoyed at the lack of cooperation—the moon did not respond. It remained completely indifferent. Tad frowned and scowled, but to no avail.

"Hell with it," he muttered. "Moon or no moon, I'm still goin'."

Then Walt came into his thoughts and he found himself grinning at the expression on Walt's face.

"He sure looked at me funny-like," he mused. Then the grin vanished. "And now that I think of it, leastways the more I think of it, the more it makes me wonder if he didn't figger I wasn't just goin' out f'r a ride. Still, I couldn't come right out with it and say, 'Look, Walt, me an' Priddy are wagin' a private war b'sides the other one. One o' his hired hands walloped me over the head t'night an' now, I'm gonna wallop Priddy. Get the idea, huh?"

He rode on for a time, hunched forward in the saddle.

"My Pop wouldn't've had t' ask 'ny questions or even look at me to know what I was up to," he continued presently. "He always seemed t' know what was in everybody else's mind and doggone it if he didn't always call the turn. I suppose if it was him in the barn t'night, 'stead o' Walt, he'da said the minute I come in there, 'Son, you figgered out yet what this other feller's gonna do once you do what you're settin' out to do? Maybe you oughtn't do it till you've kinda figgered out everything he c'n do in r'turn.' Hell!"

He was grim-faced now as he thought of Priddy.

"I'll figger the angles as I come to 'em," he muttered stubbornly. "Priddy can do anything he likes. On'y I'm gonna take a whack at him ever doggoned night, just t' pay him back. So

I won't be so all-fired smart. I'll be the dumb one but Priddy'll know he ain't up against a soft touch. I'll give him wallop f'r wallop and then we'll see who c'n take it and still keep comin' back f'r more!"

It was probably twenty minutes later when Mike brought him to the very spot on which Curly Walker had crouched earlier. Tad's keen eyes ranged over the place.

"Uh-huh," he told himself, "there's the house, and it's dark. And there's the bunkhouse and it's dark, too. The corral oughta be 'bout midway between the big house and the bunkhouse. Wa-al, there's the layout and now we'll go see what we c'n do t' give Mister Priddy somethin' t' think about."

Mike carried him in a roundabout way to lower ground. The mare was finally left in the shadows behind the bunkhouse, then Tad, bending low, went off on foot. He tripped over something, cursed softly, stopped and nudged the object with his boot toe. It was a coil of rope, forgotten by someone and left there. He bent down, caught up the coil and slung it over his shoulder. Quietly he inched his way around the bunkhouse, stopped again when he came to the window. He dropped the rope on the ground, fumbled with it for a moment until he found a loose end. The window, he had already noted, was a shutter type affair, with a heavy iron ring, evidently for a lock, where the two parts met. Deftly he slid the end of the rope through the ring, closing off the window as a means of exit, then he crept forward to the door, and quickly looped the rope around the knob. He jerked the line taut, then playing it out he backtracked, circling the building from the opposite side, and concluding again at the door where the free end of the rope was knotted around the knob.

"There," he muttered with satisfaction. "When Priddy's hired hands try t' bust outta there, they're gonna find th'mselves there to stay."

He turned, seeking the corral. He spotted it almost at once. It was some fifty feet away, and probably a hundred feet from the ranchhouse itself. The corral bars, worn smooth, gleamed like polished rifle barrels in the moonlight. His eyes widened as he stared into the enclosure. The corral was empty. He had planned to drive Priddy's horses out of the corral, send them dashing onto the range; recapturing them would have been a superhuman job for Priddy's men, who would have to had to pursue their horses on foot. Tad felt an emptiness within him. His plan had failed, and Priddy, who had struck the first blow in their private war, appeared now to have gotten away with a whole skin. Tad turned, looked questioningly and wonderingly at the silent and darkened bunkhouse. It was unusual for a ranch to be left completely alone and unguarded. It was long past the hour for everyone to be still in town. He puzzled over it, thought about it for a while; finally he shrugged his shoulder and trudged back, past the bunkhouse, and into the shadows behind it where he had left Mike.

He climbed up on her back, wheeled her, stopped her when a cold fear gripped him. Could it be that Priddy, flushed with his initial "triumph," had gone back to eke out a second one?

He jerked the reins and Mike jogged away. This time though they did not circle the place; there was no need for it since there was evidently no one at home. They clattered past the bunkhouse, then the corral, and Tad, turning briefly, glared at it as they moved past it, then they came abreast of the ranchhouse. Mechanically, Tad's eyes turned toward it. A window at the front of the house was suddenly flung open.

"Who's that?" a man's voice demanded. "Huh?"

Tad scowled darkly but he did not reply.

"Won't answer, hey?" the man's voice cried. "Awright. Mebbe this'll teach you s'me manners!"

A gun roared suddenly with a rolling thunder and a bullet kicked up a swirl of dirt just ahead of Mike. The mare cried out, and Tad, jerking out his gun, twisted around and snapped a random shot in reply, firing by instinct rather than at a definite target. He caught a fleeting glimpse of a man's head and shoulders outlined against the upper pane of a window and he fired a second time. There was a deafening, shattering crash as the pane of glass fell in. When he looked again, the man had disappeared. Tad grunted, holstered his gun and rode on. There was a barn a short distance away and Tad pulled up in front of it out of sheer curiosity. He was certain that the Priddy punchers' horses would not be found in the barn for he knew that punchers never stabled their horses save in the wintertime. He dismounted, loosened his gun in his holster for instant use, tramped up to the building and peered in. He stood in the doorway for a moment or two, listening. There was no sound from within the barn and he turned away, went back to Mike, vaulted into the saddle and rode northward.

CHAPTER SIX

Walt Walker, his rifle cradled in his arms, stopped his aimless wandering about, his sauntering in and out of the barn, and his brief halting and lounging in the open doorway of the building. He backed against the barn wall, squatted down on his heels, laid his rifle across his knees, pushed his hat up from his eyes and sighed deeply. He was tired and annoyed and he cursed the man who was responsible for causing him to lose his sleep.

"Priddy," he muttered. "I'd like to bust him a good one right smack in th' nose. On account o' him I gotta lose my good sleep."

He wondered what time it was, glanced skyward mechanically, just as he had done at least a dozen times before in the last hour. The moon was round and full and bright, and he eyed it without any display of interest or enthusiasm. The sky was equally bright, alive with stars; the fact or the possibility that he had never seen so many before left him unimpressed. He was tired, and when he needed sleep nothing could make up for it. He heard something in the distance, and he raised his head and listened briefly; presently he decided it was Tad returning from his ride. He yawned and stretched, then he yawned a second time.

He heard something again. This time it was louder; however since he already decided it was Tad, he thought no more about it. He climbed stiffly to his feet. He forgot about his rifle and it slid off his knees to the ground and he bent down and picked it up and slung it over his shoulder. It was lots easier than carrying it under his right arm or cradled in both arms. He sauntered around the barn, glanced at the house. He blinked, stopped in his tracks, stared hard, for halfway between the barn and the house were the shadowy figures of two men.

"Hey!" he sputtered and he jerked the rifle off his shoulder, threw it up.

Two Colts roared in unison; two shots were fired so close together that they blended and sounded like one. Walt gasped breathlessly, staggered away from the barn. He tottered drunkenly, suddenly dropped his rifle. He swayed, managed to steady himself somehow, and straightened up just when it appeared that he was going to fall. He turned slowly, fell against the barn wall. Slowly, awkwardly he raised his hands, cupped them around his mouth.

"Dan!" he choked.

One of the Colts thundered a second time, briefly, but with overpowering finality. The bullet slammed into Walt's body with a curious splat. Actually it sounded like a leaden slug being fired into a log. He gasped aloud. For a moment he seemed to be fighting for his breath; when it appeared that he had gotten it, he simply stiffened and pitched forward on his face. His right arm, outflung, did not move. There was a hushed silence, a heavy oppressive stillness that seemed to stifle every possible sound save the faint, fading echo of gunfire that lingered in the night air for a second or two, and then died out completely. The back door was suddenly flung open. Framed in the open doorway, and silhouetted by the light from a hastily turned-up lamp in the room behind him, stood a gaunt man with a half-raised rifle gripped in his hands. It was Pa Walker. He peered into the night.

"Walt!" he called. "You all right?"

There was no response. He plunged out of the house and the door swung and slammed behind him. He ran up the path that led to the barn, skidded to a startled, stumbling stop when the shadows of two men fell across the path. He looked up quickly, jerked his rifle upward. A Colt exploded almost in his face and he dropped the rifle. He staggered backward, stopped. He seemed to sense that another shot was coming and he threw up his right hand in a pleading gesture.

"Don't!" he panted.

The Colt roared spitefully, deafeningly. A sob broke from Pa Walker. He turned slowly, trampled himself, tottered away brokenly. He stopped again shortly, sagged and toppled over sideways.

The two men turned toward the house, but halted in surprise when they realized that someone had turned out the kitchen light. They moved closer to each other, evidently each sought the advice of the other. They backed off together, stopped again, indicating that they were still uncertain about their next move. Then a heavy rifle crashed from the window near the door and one of the shadowy figures cried out, clutched at himself and fell. His companion stood his ground for just one minute, emptying his Colt at the house in a blind, inaccurate rage. When his gun was emptied, he wheeled and bolted away. The rifle boomed a second time and the running man stumbled and fell, forced himself up to his hands and knees, then he collapsed limply. Now other men appeared out of nowhere, men who fired from the hip and whose bullets splintered the back door and shattered the window frame and pane and smashed the glass into thousands of tinkling bits. But now two other rifles, summoned to the defense of the homestead, added their voices to the din.

The attackers were forced to give ground and they retreated, but presently they came surging forward again, shooting and yelling and cursing as they advanced in a full assault upon the house. A deadly, withering flame of rifle fire burst upon them, caught them in its midst, hurled them to the ground broken, bloodied and bullet-riddled. A mere handful survived and they wheeled in disorder and fled.

Rifle-armed men poured out of the house, pursued the fleeing raiders, who sought frantically to put distance between themselves and the infuriated homesteaders. The pursuit ended shortly, evidence that the fleeing men had managed to reach their horses and thus effect their escape. The pursuers came trooping back to find Eve and Doreen sobbing hysterically over the dead bodies of Walt and Pa Walker.

It was some ten minutes later when Tad Cole rode up. He had heard the echo of crashing rifle fire. Riding Mike at break-neck pace, he came whirling up to the barn, pulled the panting mare to a skidding, stiff-legged stop, and flung himself out of the saddle. He came dashing over to the group standing between the two bodies. He collided with a husky man who pushed him off angrily. It was Allen Clark.

"What in blazes has been goin' on around here?" he demanded.

Clark eyed him coldly, hostilely.

"So the hero's fin'lly come back," he said. "What kept you, Mister Cole? Lose your way or did you stay away purposely?"

"Why, you—"

"Heroes," the man continued scornfully. "They're all alike. No guts when the chips are down. You ain't 'ny diff'rent fr'm the others I've met up with. You're all mouth and no belly f'r takin' it. G'wan, climb back up on that horse o' yourn an' get outta here!"

"Gimme a hand here, Allie," Dan Walker said over his shoulder. "Wanna get th'm into the house."

Clark turned away. Dan and he lifted the lifeless body of Pa Walker and started off with it toward the house. Eve, who was still sobbing, followed behind them. When Eddie and Curly bent over Walt, Tad stepped forward.

"Hold it a minute," he said. "Better let me give you fellers a hand."

Eddie turned his head and looked at him.

"Don't bother y'self," he said coldly. "We c'n handle it ourselves."

Tad shrugged his shoulder and stepped back. The two boys struggled manfully, managed to lift their brother's body; then they trudged away with it. Doreen had stopped crying. She bent down, picked up Walt's rifle then she caught up her father's and went striding down the path to the house. Tad turned away. He did not hear the door close behind Doreen. He went back to Mike, gripped the reins, caught the saddle horn with his free hand and swung himself up into the saddle. He wheeled the mare and rode off.

It was probably fifteen minutes later when Curly emerged from the house. He seemed surprised to find Tad gone. He ran to the barn, peered in; there was no sign there of Mike and he shook his head. Slowly he trudged down the path, stopped once and looked back. Presently he went on again, continued on into the house.

The swinging ceiling lamp in Sheriff Blix Higgins' office cast yellowish rays over the walls and made the faces of the three men sitting beneath it look unusually pale and drawn. Higgins, whose bulk overflowered his chair, sat on one side of the table; Judge Bailey and Vance Cummings sat opposite him. There was no conversation among them at the moment. They had been sitting there for almost an hour, and now it was nearly eleven o'clock and they were tired. From time to time the judge looked at his watch and each time the frown on his face deepened a little bit more. Cummings showed more patience. When the judge snapped open his heavy gold watch case and announced the time, Cummings merely listened but made no comment. Even Higgins, long since grown accustomed to being kept waiting by those to whom he owed his election to office and his continuance as sheriff, showed signs of tiring.

"I sure wish he'd come," he muttered.

He looked up when he heard Judge Bailey snap open his watch.

"What's it now, Judge?" he asked.

"It's exactly eleven o'clock," Bailey answered. "I'll give him just five minutes more, then I'm going home."

Cummings shifted himself slightly. Higgins eyed him curiously.

"Y'know," he said and Cummings looked at him. "You look like you could sit there f'rever an' never show 'ny signs o' getting tired. How d'you do it?"

The county attorney smiled patiently.

"O-h, there's no great secret about it," he replied. "I keep myself in pretty good condition so a late night here and there doesn't bother me."

"Yeah, but sometimes when I pass your place an' look up, and most o' the time it's a heap later'n it is now, there's always a light."

"I read a lot," Cummings explained. "It's education of course, but I find that it's relaxing, too. You ought to try it sometime. You might be surprised at the results."

Judge Bailey grunted. The sheriff looked at him.

"S'matter?" Higgins asked. "Don't you think I can read?"

"I don't know. Can you?"

Higgins grinned sheepishly.

"Some," he admitted.

"That's about what I thought," the judge said dryly.

He got to his feet and sauntered to the window and peered out. After a minute he turned away, retraced his steps to his chair, moved it a bit further away from the table. There was a sudden clatter of hoofs. All three looked up.

"There's Ben now," Higgins said and he sat back in his chair.

The hoofbeats swelled, then almost at once came to a full stop. There was a step outside, and the door opened. Ben Priddy stood in the doorway.

"Look here, Priddy," Judge Bailey began.

The cattleman closed the door, hitched up his belt and strode forward to the table.

"Get another chair, Blix," he said.

"Ain't got 'ny more," Higgins answered. Priddy looked at him and the burly sheriff colored and climbed to his feet. "Here, take mine. I've been sittin' all night."

"Thanks," Priddy said. He came around the table and seated himself in Higgins' chair, then he looked up at Judge Bailey. "What were you sayin' when I came in?"

The judge frowned again, jerked his chair around and sat down.

"I didn't expect t' be this late," Priddy began. "Had some bus'ness to take care of but it took longer'n I figgered it would."

"Obviously," the judge said dryly. "In the future, I'd suggest daytime meetings."

"I've got things t' do in the daytime," Priddy replied.

"So have we," Bailey said.

Priddy's mouth seemed to tighten a bit.

"Bailey." he said evenly. "And this goes f'r the rest o' you fellers, too. You fellers are workin' f'r me and when I send word that I'm comin' into town, you be where you're told t' be and on time, too. What's more, I don't want 'ny dirty looks fr'm any o' you if I'm late. Might be a good idea f'r you fellers t' kinda r'member that I put you into office an' that I c'n throw you out, too. So if you're as smart as you'd like me t' think you are, watch your step. Savvy?"

Judge Bailey coughed behind an upraised hand. Sheriff Higgins looked very unhappy and very ill at ease. He wiped his mouth with the back of his hand, spied a tiny, inoffensive speck of dust perched in the very middle of a gravy stain on his shirt-front, and scowling darkly, drew back his hand and slapped the speck off. Of the three hirelings, only Cummings sat unmoved. His steady eyes did not waver before Priddy's. Higgins cleared his throat nervously.

"What'd you have on your mind t'night, Ben?" he asked, anxious to change the unpleasant topic of Priddy's caustic remarks.

"Must've been doggoned important or you wouldn't've wanted us."

Ben Priddy grunted.

"I sent some o' my boys over to the Walker place t'night," he began.

Higgins' eyebrows arched.

"O-h, yeah?"

"Yeah," Priddy said curtly. "Cost me six men."

The sheriff whistled softly.

"Wow," he said. "Them danged homesteaders must've been all set f'r you. Get any o' them?"

"Two o' th'm," the cattleman said grimly. "The old man an' one o' his sons."

Cummings had listened attentively; he was still silent when Priddy finished his recital. Judge Bailey shook his head.

"That's bad," he said heavily. "Very bad."

Priddy's lips thinned again.

"I don't need you t' tell me that," he said coldly. "But now that you know about it, do somethin' and do it pronto."

"Just what would you like us to do?" Bailey asked. "According to your own admissions, your men attacked them."

"So what?" Priddy demanded wrathfully. "What's that gotta do with it?"

"Everything," Bailey answered. "If they killed your men in an attack upon their homestead, I'm very much afraid the law—"

"Law?" Priddy repeated as though he had never heard the word before. "Law?"

Bailey nodded mutely.

"What law?" the irate rancher fairly screamed. "I make the laws 'round here. If we haven't got one t' cover this, get busy an' get one down on the books. What'n hell d'you fellers think I pay you for, huh? To sit there an' tell me about th' law or t' do somethin' when I want somethin' done?"

Bailey took out his handkerchief, mopped his damp brow with it.

"Get this," Priddy snapped. "And get it right. I want warrants made out chargin' the Walkers, those uv 'em who are still alive, with murder. You, Higgins…"

Blix Higgins swallowed hard.

"Yeah, Ben?"

"Soon's those warrants are made out, you go serve 'em. I want those homesteaders 'rrested right off. Understand?"

Higgins gulped painfully.

"I don't aim t' lose 'ny more o' my men," Priddy continued. "You round up a posse an' do the job."

"What—whatever you say, Ben."

Priddy smiled coldly.

"Course if you hafta kill 'ny o' the Walkers while you're arrestin' them," he said, "that'll be awright, too. Just so long's you get th'm all and clear th'm off the place. O-h, yeah, Blix, I want th' kid, that Curly alive, leastways f'r a while anyway. Get it? When I'm finished with him, I'll fix him good."

He climbed to his feet, hitched up his gun belt.

"The warrants'll make everything look right, so take care o' th'm, Bailey. You, Cummings…."

The county attorney looked up at him.

"Yes?"

Ben Priddy frowned with annoyance.

"What'n hell's the matter with you?" he demanded. "You haven't said a single word."

Cummings smiled patiently.

"There wasn't any need for me to speak," he said calmly. "You seemed to have the situation pretty well in hand, so I simply listened. I don't believe you need worry. We've done your bidding before. We've had men convicted and hung, just as you ordered. And since you want the surviving Walkers hung, doubtless they'll be hung."

Priddy seemed relieved.

"That's better," he said.

Cummings shifted himself a bit.

"Of course," he began again, "the fact that the Walkers had every right to defend themselves in whatever way they could, we-ll, we won't pay any attention to that. The point is you want them hung, so that will more than suffice for any lawful and legal reason."

"Wait a minute," Priddy said darkly. "What are you tryin' t' hand me, huh?"

"Nothing," Cummings said evenly. "I merely made a statement of fact, and that was all."

Ben Priddy leaned over the table.

"Y'know, Mister," he said. "This ain't the first time I've had reason t' wonder if it was smart o' me t' give you a job instead o' lettin' you starve t' death."

Vance Cummings laughed softly.

"And I've never gotten over debating the wisdom of accepting a job from you," he said. "Doubtless I wouldn't have had the material things I have now, but I know I'd have had a much easier time of living with myself if I had turned down your offer."

Priddy drew a deep breath.

"I've got this much more t' say to you, Cummings," he said with finality. "I don't like you overmuch, but if you stay in line, keep your mouth shut an' do's you're told, you got a pretty good chance o' dyin' a natural death. But you try crossin' me just once. You'll wind up with a slug right smack in your gizzard an' that'll be that. Do I make myself clear, Mister Cummings?"

"Perfectly clear."

"Awright then. You fellers know what I want done. See that it's done."

There was a moment's silence, then Priddy straightened up, kicked his chair out of the way, and went storming out of the office. The door swung swiftly behind him, slammed shut. Cummings laughed again and got to his feet.

"Coming, Judge?" he asked.

Bailey was mopping his brow again.

"Presently," he answered. He pocketed his handkerchief, shook his head sadly. "The man's mad, I tell you. Stark mad."

"I don't think so," Cummings said. "He rides roughshod over everyone because he knows there's no one to stop him."

"That's right," Higgins said.

Cummings turned, looked at him for a moment.

"You, Sheriff, appear to have drawn the worst assignment of all."

"Damned right," Higgins said gloomily. "Doggone it, I wish t' hell I could take this star o' mine and chuck it outta the window."

"You know of course what that would get you—don't you?"

"Sure. A good solid hunk o' lead."

"Exactly. And to quote Mister Priddy, if I may, right smack in your rather ample gizzard."

The sheriff grinned sheepishly.

"Sometimes I think it'd be a doggoned cheap price t' pay f'r gettin' away fr'm him," he said. "Come on, you fellers. Let's get outta here. I'm gonna get me a bottle o' somethin' an' take it t' bed with me. That's a sure way o' sleepin' without bein' disturbed by Ben Priddy."

CHAPTER SEVEN

I t was two days after the raid that Tad rode slowly through the grove of trees that fringed the northern tip of the Walker place. He had been there on each of the nights after the raid, too, determined to exact a fair share of Priddy blood should the cattleman and his punchers attempt another attack. But much to his annoyance, the Priddy outfit did not appear, and he grumbled about it and cursed them roundly. Now it was early morning, and his disposition was none too good. The sun was bright and warm and cheerful, but he glowered at it one moment, and disregarded it the next. He had stumbled across a thicket about a mile away that provided him with an excellent "holing up" spot, with thick brush all around to screen him from probing, seeking eyes, and an excellent jumping-off point for his nighttime sallies. He belched and made a wry face. The coffee he had prepared for his breakfast hadn't smelled too good—it had tasted even worse. Now the mere thought of it sickened him.

Then, too, he was tired of living under cover. True, his blankets were warm and thick but they couldn't begin to compare with a bed. His back and neck muscles were sore, and every time he turned or made a sudden movement, the stiffened muscles protested and made him wince.

"Damn," he muttered. "How in hell do I manage t' get into these things, huh? 'Stead o' livin' like other folks do, I hafta hole up like a gopher. Now I feel like a team o' mules've been yankin' me from both ends, I'm so doggoned stiff an' sore. I sure wish I could run into that ornery Ben Priddy out by 'imself f'r his mornin' ride. Bet I could do one swell job on him, judging by the way I feel right now.

The grass beneath Mike's hoofs was young and fresh and sweet-smelling and the breath of it carried up to Tad's nostrils. He sniffed it once, frowned, refused to permit its sweetness to effect his over-all feeling. Mike stopped suddenly and Tad who hadn't been too alert up to the moment was jolted so forcibly that he fell forward against the mare's stiffened neck.

"Damn it, Mike!" he exploded. "What in blazes—" He stopped abruptly, raised his eyes. Standing a dozen feet ahead of them, a leveled rifle in his hands, was Allen Clark. "Oh," Tad said significantly. "It's you."

The muzzle of Clark's rifle gaped at Tad's chest but the lean youth merely glanced at it, then he looked down at the husky man behind the rifle.

"Thought I told you t' get the hell away fr'm here," Clark said gruffly. "And t' stay away."

Tad eased himself in the saddle.

"That was th' other night," he said calmly. "This is t'day."

Clark's lips tightened.

"Turn around and get outta here," he commanded.

Tad shook his head.

"Nope," he answered.

Their eyes met for a moment, and clashed. Allen grunted finally, lowered his rifle and put it down on the ground, then he picked it up again and stood it up against a tree.

"Awright," he said. "I've been hopin' I'd get another chance t' tangle with you, hero. Didn't figger I'd be so lucky so soon. Climb down, mister. You an' me've got some unfinished bus'ness to attend to."

"You learn th' hard way, don't you?"

Clark did not answer. He turned away, unbuttoned and rolled up his sleeves, turned around again.

"Well?" he demanded presently. "Do I hafta haul you down or c'n you make it by y'self?"

Tad dismounted. He took off his hat, put it down on the ground, unbuckled and removed his gun belt and stowed it away under the hat. This time he did not take off his shirt; he simply wiped his hands on it, flexed his fingers. He glanced at Mike, and the mare, watching him, promptly backed away.

"Well?" Clark demanded again.

He suddenly realized that he hadn't taken off his hat, and he whipped it off, tossed it aside.

"Come on," he commanded and put up his hands.

Tad came plunging forward. Clark was not prepared for such a maneuver; he had expected Tad to move in cautiously, with his left hand thrust out. He was still setting himself, planting his feet solidly on the ground, when Tad's left fist exploded in his face with the report of a touched-off firecracker, and with stunning force. Allen staggered back. A second punch landed squarely on his nose and mouth, and blood spurted out of one nostril and from his smashed lips. He was a bit dazed from the effect of the two blows when Tad's left made a return appearance. It went straight through Clark's open guard and collided head-on with his right eye. That was the beginning of the end, for when Allen squared off again, his right eye had begun to close.

He bulled his way forward doggedly, grunting and blowing, sighted his tormentor and swung viciously and desperately. Tad side-stepped and the force and momentum of Clark's wild swing carried him a full step past Tad. As he turned around a flurry of punches greeted him, staggered him again and made him stumble about helplessly. His right eye was tightly closed, and an angry-looking welt under his left eye heralded an early closing of that eye, too. He thrust out his arms, groped for something to hold on to. He tried to back Tad into a sturdy tree trunk, seeking evidently to clutch his agile opponent in this thick arms, but

Tad pushed him away, lashed out at him, and struck him several times in the face. Clark rocked under the impact of Tad's blows. Finally he sagged and collapsed in a battered heap. He rolled over on his broad back.

"Come on," Tad panted. "You asked f'r this, so get up and take it."

There was no more fight left in Allen Clark. He lay sprawled out on the ground with both of his arms out-flung. His face was bloodied, battered and swollen. After a minute Tad lowered his fists, unclenched them and stepped back. He looked at his knuckles. There was blood on them and he bent down, wiped his hands on the grass; when he came erect again he smoothed down his hair, tucked his shirttail into his pants.

"Well, Mister Clark?" he asked.

There was no response. Tad donned his hat, buckled on his gun belt. Mike came forward now and Tad vaulted up on her back. He did not even look down at Clark as he rode past. Minutes later Mike carried him out of the woods. They loped along the fringe of the Walker fields, slowed to a jog as they came up to the barn. Tad pulled Mike to a full stop when he saw the kitchen door open. As he watched, a slim, girlish figure in dungarees backed out. It was Eve. When she turned around he saw that she was carrying a heavy bucket. She caught the swinging door with a backward thrust of her foot, checked it, then she let it close. She started up the path, stopped to shift the bucket to her other hand. He frowned, swung himself off Mike's back, hitched up his pants, then he came striding down the path to meet her. He stopped in front of her; she stopped, too, raised her eyes to his. For a brief moment they looked at each other. Her eyes were heavy-lidded and he noticed a curious and unfamiliar tightening around the corners of her mouth. He reached for the bucket, took it from her, turned abruptly and started away. She followed at his heels, then she quickened her pace and marched along at his side.

"I—I thought you'd gone," she said.

"I've been aroun' here all the time," he answered without looking at her.

"Oh."

"I've been here every night, too," he added.

Out of the corner of his eye he saw her look up at him.

"Doreen's going home," she said shortly. "To Grandfather's."

He made no comment.

"Eddie and Allen Clark are going with her," she continued.

They came around the barn to the open doorway of the building and they halted there.

"And you're stayin' on?" he asked.

"Yes. So are Dan and Curly. We tried to talk Curly into going back with Doreen but he wouldn't hear of it."

Tad put down the bucket.

"Maybe if you'd go back, he'd go, too," he suggested.

She shook her head.

"But I don't want to go back. We came out here for good, and I want to stay."

"When's Doreen plannin' to go?"

"Today," she replied. "She's packing her things now. Just as I came out of the house, I heard Dan tell Curly to hitch up the wagon."

"H'm," she heard him say.

"What's the matter?"

There was a small pail standing just inside the doorway. He caught it up, looked in it. It was empty. He poured some of the water into it from the bucket.

"Keep a towel out here, don't you?" he asked.

"Yes. Just inside, on the wall to the left."

He found the towel hanging on a nail, snatched it off and slung it over his shoulder. He picked up the pail. She looked at him curiously, questioningly.

"Look," he said. "I'll be back in a little while."

"Where are you going?" she asked. "And what are those things for?"

"Tell you all about it later on," he promised.

"We-ll—"

He stepped past her, went striding away. Water from the pail, swinging against his thigh, sloshed over his right pants leg, and he stopped. She heard him voice an annoyed "Damn," saw him shift the pail to his left hand and hold the pail just a bit more securely, then he tramped off. Mike had turned her head; she watched him for another minute, then she simply jogged after him, overtook him shortly. Tad stopped a second time, when the mare clattered up to him. He gripped the saddle horn with his right hand, pulled himself up astride Mike, settled himself, then holding the pail out at arm's length, rode away. Eve carried the bucket into the barn.

Allen Clark was up on his feet—actually he was standing on widespread legs—when Tad rode up to him. Allen did not raise his head. He busied himself tucking in his shirttails. Tad dismounted, trudged over to him, set the pail down on the grass.

"Understand you're goin' away with Doreen and Eddie," he said. "Accordin' to Eve, Doreen's packin'. You oughta make y'self kinda pr'sentable y'know b'fore she comes lookin' for you."

Clark's head came up. He glared at Tad through his swollen left eye. The right eye was tightly closed. Tad grinned at him.

"H-m," he said. "I sure did a job on you, awright. Guess I don't even know m' own strength. Gonna hafta watch myself fr'm now on. Can't let m'self get riled up again. I'm liable to f'rget that I'm hell-on-wheels and actu'lly tear somebody apart, and doggone it, that'd never do, y'know. O-h, here's a towel."

He whipped it off his shoulder, and tossed it into Clark's hands.

"If I were you," he continued, "I'd wet one end of it good and lay it first on one eye, then the other."

Allen knelt down on the grass. His movements were stiff, almost painful. He thrust one end of the towel into the water, held it there for a moment, then he carried it up to his right eye.

"That's the idea," Tad said, watching him. "Look, you keep on like you're doin' and fix y'self up. I'm goin' back. If I see Doreen, I'll tell her you'll be along d'rectly. O-h, yeah, Clark, when you put your hat on, kinda jerk it down over your eyes. Get the idea? 'Course once you're on your way and Doreen keeps askin' what happened t' you, you oughta be able t' cook up some yarn t' tell her. You c'n even make y'self a hero if you like. Nob'dy'll know the difference."

He grinned again, turned on his heel and went back to Mike. He vaulted into the saddle, wheeled the mare.

"Be seein' you," he called over his shoulder, then he spurred Mike and sent her dashing away. He twisted around once and looked back. Clark was still kneeling over the pail of water. Tad shook his head. "Wonder if anybody'd b'lieve me if I told th'm that first I beat up the feller, and than then I go get 'im water and a towel and tell 'im how t' fix himself up. It even sounds cockeyed t' me. I ain't so sure that I'd believe it if somebody else told it t' me."

There was a wagon drawn up in front of the barn when he came in sight of it again. He saw Eddie emerge, leading two horses. Dan appeared at that moment, too, and together they backed the horses into the traces, hitched them in their places. Then he saw Doreen. She was wearing a big hat and there were gay feathers on it. Dan lifted her onto the wide drivers' seat. Tad clattered up, reined in, and Dan turned. He nodded to Tad. No one said anything. Doreen busied herself smoothing down the front of her dress, Eddie trudged around to the rear of the wagon, then Dan came around, too, to join him. Together they hoisted a huge trunk, then a slightly smaller one, into the wagon. Tad eased himself in the saddle. Presently Dan and Eddie tramped forward again.

"Tad," Dan said. "See anything o' Allen Clark?"

"Huh? Oh, sure. Told me t' tell you he'd be along d'rectly."

Dan gave him a curious look but he said nothing. Eve came out of the barn. She stopped in the doorway, leaned back against the door frame. Doreen raised her eyes; they met Tad's for a moment, then they shifted, went past him. It was probably five minutes later when Eddie nudged Dan.

"There's Allie now," he said.

Everyone's eyes turned to follow Eddie's pointing finger. Eddie wheeled suddenly and strode back to Eve. He stopped in front of her. He bent suddenly and kissed her soundly on the cheek, wheeled, and scampered back to the wagon, climbed up beside Doreen. Allen Clark came closer. Tad turned his head. He looked in Eve's direction. He was surprised to find that she had disappeared. Clark passed within arm's reach of Mike and Tad glanced at him and smiled inwardly when he saw that the man had acted on his suggestion—the brim of his hat was pulled down far over his face, shading his battered eyes. In addition, Clark now whipped out his handkerchief, a huge, colorful bandanna, opened it, and he seemed to be trying to wipe his face from ear to ear in one general, two-handed movement. He stopped in front of Dan, thrust out his right hand. Dan gripped it but before he could say anything, Clark withdrew his hand, turned and climbed up on the driver's seat. Hastily he crumpled his bandanna, shoved it into his pants pocket, turned up his shirt collar all around, grabbed the reins, and settled himself far back on the seat. When Doreen looked at him, he jerked his hat brim even farther down.

"All set?" he asked in a voice that seemed unfamiliar.

"Yep," Eddie said. "G'bye!"

"Hold it a minute," Dan said. He came striding around the horses to the other side of the wagon, mounted the wheel, and leaned over Eddie, Doreen bent toward him, kissed him, then she bowed her head and dabbed at her eyes with a tiny square of linen that made Tad feel certain it could never prove equal to any need, most certainly not one of a practical nature. Dan rumpled Eddie's hair.

"Take care o' your sister, young feller," he said. "And take care o' yourself, too. Understand?"

Eddie swallowed hard. He tried to answer but his efforts proved futile; however, he did manage a clumsy, gulping nod, and Dan patted him on the head. Dan jumped down, stepped back. Clark released the hand brake; it squeaked dismally, then the horses moved away.

"G'bye!" Dan yelled. "G'bye!"

They heard Clark's voice. The horses responded by quickening their pace. They watched the wagon until it disappeared from sight, then Dan, standing a dozen feet away from Tad, drew a deep breath.

"We-ell," he said and there was both sadness and marked heaviness in his voice. "That's that."

He turned and looked toward the doorway.

"She's prob'bly inside," Tad said.

Dan nodded, trudged into the barn. Tad swung himself out of the saddle. Minutes later Dan sauntered out. He stopped, looked at Tad.

"You plannin' t' stay here?" he asked.

"I'd like to stay," Tad answered. "That is, if you want me to."

"Can't offer you anything," Dan said, " 'cept maybe a chance t' wind up with one o' Priddy's slugs in your belly."

"I'm willin' to take that chance."

Dan shrugged his broad shoulders.

"Awright," he said. "You're hired. Better put your horse in the barn. You won't be doin' any ridin' f'r a while. Then you'd better come into th' house and eat somethin'. We c'n all stand some grub. Maybe it'll make us feel better. I don't mind sayin' that right now I feel lower'n I've ever felt b'fore."

He plodded away toward the house.

"Go 'head," he said over his shoulder. "I'll get the coffee goin' meanwhile."

"Right."

Tad watched him for a moment, saw him go into the house, then he turned toward Mike, stopped and looked at the house again. He hadn't noticed it before, but the door was a new one, a newer, brighter, cleaner wood than the rest of the house, and when his eyes strayed past it to the window he noticed something there, too. There was no glass in the window frame. There were a dozen black holes at various points around the window and he studied them briefly before he realized what they were.

"Bullet holes," he muttered. "Souvenirs fr'm the other night."

He led Mike into the barn. There was a mound of hay in a shadowy corner and perched on it was Eve. He glanced at her but she gave no sign of recognition. He guided the mare beyond the hay mound, unsaddled her, patted her rump, then he tramped out.

When he entered the house Dan looked up.

"Eve comin' in?" he asked.

"Dunno," Tad answered. He took off his hat, dropped it into a chair near the door. "I didn't ask her. She was sitting out there on s'me hay and she looked like she didn't want to be disturbed, so I kept goin' like I didn't even see her."

Dan nodded understandingly. There was a moment in a far corner of the room, and Tad turned. It was Curly. He was sitting astride a chair. Tad nodded to him. The boy did not acknowledge Tad's nod; instead, he got to his feet and went out. Dan and Tad looked at each other, and Dan simply shook his head.

"Sit down," he said. "Take any chair you like."

CHAPTER EIGHT

Ben Priddy had had a restless night. When he arose the next morning and started down the stairs, he was mumbling to himself. Turning from the foot of the stairs into the short, narrow hallway that led to the kitchen, he tripped over the curled-up end of the faded carpet.

"Damnation!" he roared. He drew back, launched a vicious kick at the offending strip of carpeting, missed and wound up by kicking himself in the ankle of his pivoting left foot.

Martha Priddy was setting the kitchen table for breakfast when she heard her husband's voice. She went to the doorway and peered into the hall. Ben caught sight of her, and he came storming toward her.

"Damnation, Martha!" he sputtered angrily. "How many times do I hafta tell you t' have that danged thing nailed down b'fore I break my neck, huh?"

Martha and Ben Priddy had been married for twenty-seven years. In that time Martha had learned much about men, but she had learned even more about one man in particular—her husband. She was quite used to his outbursts; the years had taught her how to calm him down.

"Breakfast's ready," she said, turned on her heel and retraced her steps to the table and continued setting it.

"The hell with breakfast!" he roared.

"Very well," she said calmly. "Since you don't want any suppose you go outside. I'm hungry but I don't enjoy eating with a madman ranting all over the place."

She poured coffee for herself, sat down, buttered a biscuit and proceeded with her own breakfast. Ben stalked to the table, stood over it, glowered at his wife. When she refused to look up, he swung a chair around and sat down.

"We-ll?" he demanded.

Martha drank some coffee, munched her biscuit, took another swallow of the coffee, then she raised her head.

"O-h," she said. "Change your mind?"

Ben frowned darkly.

"Come on," he said curtly. "I've got things t' do. Where's that daughter o' yourn? Doesn't she know it's time t' get up?"

"She is up," Martha said calmly. "I just heard her moving about in her room."

"Why don't she get down here t' eat when we do?"

"Because I've told her to stay upstairs till you're finished and gone."

"S'matter? Ain't I good enough f'r her t' eat with?"

"It isn't that. It's enough that I have to contend with your temper. She doesn't have to. She isn't married to you, you know. She's only your daughter and that makes a difference."

She reached for the coffee pot, handled it gingerly, filled his cup, then she put down the pot, and went on with her breakfast.

"There's somethin' the matter with that girl," he said.

"Is there? I hadn't noticed anything wrong."

Ben sipped his coffee, found it wasn't too hot, drank a mouthful.

"She moons around like a sick calf," he said presently.

"Most girls do. It isn't anything unusual."

He buttered a biscuit, stuffed it into his mouth, washed it down with some more coffee.

"Now that you've calmed down," Martha began, "there's something I want to talk to you about."

"Yeah. You don't say?"

"Yes. One of your notes is due for payment next week. What are you going to do about it?"

He put down his cup, leaned over the table.

"I'll take care of it," he said. "You leave those things t' me."

"How will you take care of it?"

"How d'you think?" he retorted.

"I don't know. I know you haven't the money, or at least I don't think you have. Of course the bank may be willing to extend the note, but I doubt it. You've never been a very prompt payer and they're probably aware of it."

"Yeah? You think you know everything, just b'cause you had a lotta schoolin' and I didn't. Lemme tell you somethin'. One o' these days I'm gonna have more dough—"

"Money."

"Dough, money, what's th' diff'rence? Like I started t' say b'fore, I'm gonna have me a heap more dough'n you ever heard of."

"Where are you going to get it?"

He glared at her.

"You c'n ask more questions th'n a lawyer."

"You haven't answered my question," she said evenly. "Where are you going to get it?"

"Where d'you think?"

"I haven't any idea."

"I made it in a deal."

"What kind of a deal?"

He frowned darkly, looked at her for a moment, pushed his chair back from the table. He started to rise but she gestured and he stopped halfway, then slowly he came erect.

"There's something else that I'd like to know about."

"Yeah?" he said belligerently, defiantly.

"I was in town the other day."

"So what?"

"I ran into Ann Pierce. We talked a while."

He grunted scornfully.

"She'd do a heap better if she stayed on the ranch 'stead o' gallivantin' here an' there all th' time. That husband o' hers needs all th' help he c'n get and he can't get any b'cause he ain't got the money f'r wages."

"I don't know anything about that. We didn't speak of it. What interested us both was your attitude toward these homesteaders. Lee Pierce doesn't want any quarrel with them. According to Ann, neither do any of the other ranchers. Just why are you persecuting them?"

"Because I hate th'm," he said loudly. "I hate their guts. That good enough reason?"

"No," she said quietly. "There must be another reason, a better one. What is it?"

"I'm a cattleman," he said, stabbing himself with his right thumb. "Them damned homesteaders move in where they ain't wanted and where they ain't got 'ny right t' be."

"Does the law say they mustn't—"

"The hell with th' law! I make my own laws, and if I wait f'r the law t' step in and see to it that nob'dy barges in on me an' cuts off some o' the land I'm usin' f'r grazing purposes, I'd be plumb outta luck."

"We-ll, who owns that land, the grazing land?"

"Nob'dy."

"Then what right have you—"

"What right?" he echoed. "I was here first. That gives me all the right in th' world t' keep it clear. You r'member a couple o' years back when Jess Vaughn—"

"I don't like that man," Martha interrupted. "And I never will."

"Nobody's asked you t' like him. I like him and that's enough f'r me. Anyway, a family o' homesteaders named Yates moved in b'tween Vaughn's place an' the river. First thing they did was t' string up a lotta wire. A dry spell come along an' Jess started t' drive his cattle toward the river. They run smack into the wire, piled up on it, and Jess lost more'n two hundred head. He went plumb loco."

"I'd expect that of him. Did the thought occur to him to go around the wire?"

"That would've taken at least another hull day. But Jess knew what t' do. When the Yates bunch wouldn't let him through—"

"I remember it now. They'd planted corn in those fields and to let the Vaughn cattle through there would have meant the corn would have been trampled and ruined."

His eyes gleamed with a steely grimness.

"Yates' wife grabbed up a rifle an' told Jess to get off the place. He did, but that night, 'long about midnight, he came back, together with a lot o' his men. They swooped down on the place, wiped it out, along with every one of the Yates family. Next mornin' Jess drove his cattle through the place and down t' the river. He sure showed them homesteaders what was what."

"Just as you're trying to show the Walkers."

"Damned right, and when I get through with th'm, b'lieve me, they'll wish t' hell they'da stayed where they belonged. This is cattle country, an' by God, we'll keep it f'r cattle. I know the West's big, but it ain't big enough f'r ranchin' and farmin' both, and since we got here first, we're gonna hold on to it."

He hitched up his pants. He looked at her, but she was silent now.

"Look," he said again. "Suppose you stick t' your knittin' and leave the runnin' o' the ranch t' me? I know what's what about it and you don't. I was raised on a ranch. It's in my blood, part o' me. Understand?"

She raised her eyes to meet his.

"I think I understand a lot of things now, Ben," she said quietly. "A lot more than I understood before."

"What's that supposed t' mean?"

"O-h, for one thing, I don't believe for a minute that that Walker boy had anything to do with the killing of the Hassetts."

"You don't, eh!"

"I think it was a trumped-up affair, from beginning to end, and the Walker boy was simply offered up as a victim. He's a homesteader and the actual killer took that into consideration together with the fact the sentiment in a cattle country would condemn him without a fair trial. Ben, I don't think you honestly believe him guilty either. There's another reason behind this business why you clamored so loudly and fought so hard to have that boy hanged. I wonder what that reason is?"

"You seem t' know all the answers," he said tauntingly. "Suppose you tell me?"

"You disliked the Hassetts, both of them. I might even say you hated them. I heard you say that any number of times."

"What's that got t' do with it?"

"It seems strange to me that when they were killed, you rose up in all your indignation and clamored the loudest that justice be done, and that the killer be brought to time."

"Sure I did, an' I'm still hllerin' f'r it."

"In all the years I've known you, you've never cared in the slightest what happened to anyone. I'll make a correction there. You've been considerate as far as I'm concerned, but that's all. Now why all this sudden feeling for the Hassetts? It doesn't ring true."

"Look," he said darkly. "This could go on f'rever. Once you get 'n idea, all hell couldn't change it. I ain't got the time t' stand here and argue. I got other things t' do, more important ones."

He turned on his heel, started out of the room.

"Ben," Martha called.

He halted when he reached the doorway, turned and looked back at her over his shoulder.

"Ben," she said again, "I want you to tell me something, and truthfully, too. You know who killed the Hassetts, don't you?"

His lips tightened, then they thinned into a straight line.

"Was it Jess Vaughn who killed them?"

The muscles in his jaws twitched.

"Don't be a damned fool!" he said gruffly.

"And that money you were talking about," she continued. "The money you're going to get."

"We-ll? What about it?"

She shook her head.

"Go on," he commanded. "I wanna hear the rest of it."

She shook her head again.

"No," she said heavily. "I think you'd better go now."

He wheeled, stormed out. Presently the front door slammed behind him. Martha got to her feet; she heard a quick step in the hallway, and she turned toward the doorway. Lila looked in.

"Father gone?" she asked.

"Didn't you hear the door?"

Lila did not answer. She came into the room, stopped in front of the table.

"I heard his voice a couple of times," she said. "He was terribly angry about something, wasn't he?"

Martha smiled patiently.

"Yes," she replied. "However, it doesn't take much to anger your father, you know, particularly when he's in the wrong."

"I know," Lila said. "But I've never seen you looking so worried. What's the matter, Mother?"

Martha smiled again. Evidently it was meant to reassure her daughter that there was nothing amiss. She leaned over the table and patted Lila's cheek.

"I didn't sleep very well last night," she said. "It was probably due to something I ate before we turned in. And at my age, you know, losing a night's sleep, we-ll, it shows and I'm afraid I can't do very much about it."

Lila seated herself, but it was immediately apparent that she was not at all satisfied with her mother's explanation. She followed

Martha's every move with anxious eyes. Martha, returning to the table with a platter of hot biscuits, found Lila watching her.

"Here," she said briskly. "They're piping hot. And if I do say so myself, they're positively the best I've ever tasted."

"Mother," Lila said. "I heard Father say something about homesteaders. Is there going to be more trouble with them?"

"Milk or coffee?" Martha asked.

"Mother!"

"Will you have milk or coffee?" Martha repeated quietly.

Their eyes met briefly; it was Lila who flushed and finally averted her eyes.

"Milk, please," she said.

"That's better."

"Father's planning something terrible again against those poor Walker people," Lila said. "Isn't he?"

Martha's eyebrows arched.

"I've never heard you say that before—'those poor Walker people,'" she commented.

Lila flushed for the second time.

"We-ell," she said a bit awkwardly. "They're people, aren't they, just like us?"

"Very much so, dear, even though your father doesn't think they are. But what's responsible for the change in feeling toward them or about them?"

"O-h, there isn't any special reason," Lila said hastily.

"Isn't there?"

Lila fingered a biscuit, turned it over in her hand.

"Don't you think you ought to tell me? You will sooner or later, you know, so why not now?"

Martha came closer, bent over her daughter, pillowed Lila's head against her shoulder.

"I'm waiting, dear."

"We-ll," Lila began.

"Y-es?"

Lila moved away a bit from her mother, turned and looked up at her.

"You're probably going to be awf'lly angry with me," she said.

"Am I?"

Lila nodded mutely.

"Try me," Martha suggested encouragingly. "Maybe you'll be agreeably surprised."

Lila lowered her eyes.

"I've been seeing that Walker boy," she said. "The one they call Curly."

Martha drew a deep breath.

"I don't mean lately," Lila added quickly, "but before."

"I see."

Lila looked up at her again.

"He's awf'lly nice," she went on. "If you could talk to him, I know you'd like him, too. He has the nicest eyes, and the nicest way of talking. But I feel simply terrible about him now."

"You mean—"

"Yes. I can imagine how he must hate us now, even me, for what happened to his father and brother. Mother, why must people go 'round killing other people, 'specially when they're such nice people, too!"

"It wouldn't do for your father to know about this, Lila," Martha said.

"I know that," Lila said miserably.

"Maybe he does know about it," a voice said from the doorway. They turned as one, aghast. Ben Priddy, his thumbs hooked in his belt, stood in the doorway. His face was grim and his eyes were cold and hard. "Anytime either o' you two think you're puttin' somethin' over on me, you've got another guess comin'."

Lila shrank back against her mother.

"I know you've been seein' that murderin' young pup," Ben went on. "But I didn't say 'nything. I wanted t' see what was gonna come of it. Now I know. You'd take sides with anybody 'gainst your father. But that's awright. I've been kinda expectin' that t' happen. Your mother's th' same way, an' you wouldn't be her daughter if you didn't feel th' way she does 'bout me. But that's awright, too. Long's I know how I stand aroun' here, I'm satisfied. On'y r'member this. You two think I've been ornery up t' now. We-ell, you watch an' see me fr'm now on."

He wheeled and went out. They heard him stride the length of the hall, heard him go upstairs; it was barely a minute later when he came down again, and presently they heard the front door open, then they heard it slam shut. Martha tiptoed to the doorway and peered into the hall. She turned slowly.

"He's gone again," she said simply.

Lila came across the room.

"What do you think he'll do?" she asked.

Martha shook her head.

"I don't know," she answered. "But if he's really as angry as I think he is, he'll have to let his feelings out on someone. He's always been like that."

Lila's eyes widened; there was a quickening in her breath.

"You mean, he'll go after the Walkers again?"

Martha nodded grimly.

"I'm afraid so."

Lila's eyes blazed.

"Then I hope they give it back to him, good," she said heatedly. "Even if he is my own father!"

It was noon and Sheriff Blix Higgins was sitting in his office, his elbows on the table, his head in his big hands. He looked worried. He heard a clatter of hoofs somewhere along the street, but he paid no further attention to it, He was concerned with a weighty problem, and the longer he pondered about it, the more sorrowful his already glum expression became. He lowered his arms, sank back in his chair and shook his head.

"Wa-al," he said with finality and resignation in his voice. "I've done 'bout all I could. 'Course I don't expect that t' satisfy him, so whatever he wants t' do about it'll be awright with me."

He brushed a smudge of dirt from his pants leg.

"He'll prob'bly come bustin' in here madder'n a wet hen," he muttered.

He closed his eyes. He heard the street door open but he did not move.

"Go 'way," he said with a gesture of his hand. "I got troubles o' my own."

He heard the door close. He opened his eyes, turned his head. He stared hard, gulped and tried to swallow but he nearly choked. Standing with his back against the closed door was a tight-lipped Ben Priddy. Blix gulped a second time and managed to swallow.

"B-Ben," he said in a tone that sounded like a wheeze. "I'm glad t' see you."

"I'll bet you are," Priddy said curtly. He came striding across the floor to the table. "Why didn't you let me know you couldn't raise a posse like I tol' you to, huh?"

"I-I-I tried, Ben."

Priddy swung a chair around, seated himself on it.

"How many men were willin' t' serve?" he asked.

"Six," Blix answered hopefully. "Honest, Ben, I argued and hollered and pleaded, but it didn't do a damn bit o' good. I dunno what's th' matter with th' men aroun' here. They used t' be ready f'r most anything th' minute I come after 'em."

"I know," Ben said, nodding. "They got walloped a little bit that night we tangled with th' Walkers, an' they ain't got guts enough t' wanna pay th'm back. Look, Blix—"

"Yeah?"

"You sure about them six?"

"I c'n get them th' minute you want th'm."

"Awright then. I got four o' my boys along with me t'day. The six you got makes ten. You an' me makes it twelve. That oughta be more'n enough t' handle any homesteader outfit."

"O-h, sure!"

" 'Long about ten o'clock," Priddy continued, "you go round up your six an' bring th'm here."

"Y'mean we're goin' after th' Walkers t'night?"

"What th' hell d'you think I'm talkin' about?" Ben demanded fiercely. "I've let them mavericks live too long a'ready. Now that I've had enough o' th'm, I'm gonna wipe 'em out."

"What time'll you be back here?"

"I'm here now," Priddy said curtly, "an' I'm stayin' in town f'r th' rest o' the day. I got some other things to attend to, an' I might's well clean 'em all up while I got th' chance. Couple o' hours oughta be all I'll need, an' fr'm then on I'll be in here markin' time 'till we're ready t' ride. An' this time, b'lieve me, th' Walkers are gonna get all th' hell I've been savin' up f'r th'm!"

"I oughta go get them warrants fr'm the judge."

"F'rget them things," Ben said. "I'll be along an' that'll be all th' law we'll need with us."

CHAPTER NINE

I t was late afternoon and now the shadowy fingers of approaching evening were flexing themselves and spreading out over the range. A lone horseman appeared on the horizon. It was "Shorty" Cahill, and his borrowed horse panted to a self-decided-upon halt atop a rise that fortunately commanded a broad view of the rolling prairie-land. Cahill offered no objection to the stop. He was glad of the chance to stand up in the stirrups, glad of the opportunity to ease himself after a jolting session astride the bony horse. It was a long time since he had done any riding; the fact that he had never possessed any mastery as a horseman, and the admission that the years between had lessened his limited skill in the saddle, had already done much to make this occasion a most painful one. He made a wry face when he stood up.

"I won't be able to sit down for a week," he muttered to himself.

Now he availed himself of the opportunity to let his eyes scan the open country on every side of him. They swept the far-spreading span of green and brown rangeland, stopped and focused on two figures that were probably half a mile away. He forgot his own soreness for a minute while he studied the pair, and he frowned when he found himself unable to identify them.

"H-m," he said finally. "Unless I'm mistaken, one of them's a girl. I wonder who she is?"

The idling horse pawed the ground impatiently and Cahill glared at him.

"O-h," he said resentfully. "So you're all ready to go again, are you? We-ll, just you take your time, my bony friend. I'll let you know when I'm ready."

He lowered himself gently into the saddle, and he grimaced again when he felt the uncompromising combination of stiff, hard leather and bony back under him. He settled himself, tightened his grip on the reins, and finally nudged his mount with his knees. The animal loped off. The grass beneath his hoofs was thick and lush and it cushioned and absorbed his hoofbeats.

"Well!" Cahill said suddenly. "From the looks of things I'd say there's a romance about to burst forth into full bloom. That's a very tender embrace, if ever I saw one."

He was some thirty feet from the pair when the girl turned her head, and saw him. She flushed, and hastily broke away from her companion and stepped back. The young man with her promptly showed his lack of experience in such sudden intrusions, for he flushed, too, stepped back awkwardly, stepped on himself in the process, then flustered, he strode hurriedly to where his horse was calmly nibbling on some fresh young grass. Cahill coughed discreetly, pulled his horse to a stop. He touched the brim of his battered hat.

"Pardon me for intruding," he said gravely, "but can you tell me—"

He stopped abruptly. The girl was Lila Priddy and he showed his surprise.

"Oh!" he said. He looked at the youth. "You're one of the Walkers, aren't you?"

Curly's right hand was curled around the butt of a Colt that jutted out of his pants belt. Cahill flashed a reassuring smile.

"My name's Cahill," he said quickly.

His introduction failed to draw a response of any kind.

"If this young lady will excuse us for a moment," he said, "I'd like a word with you."

Curly looked at him.

"It's important," Cahill added.

Curly glanced at Lila, then he looked up at Cahill again and nodded.

"Awright," he said. "But anything you've got t' say t' me, you c'n say in front o' her."

Cahill shrugged his shoulder.

"Very well," he said. "I think you'd better hustle home and get your family on the move."

Curly's lips tightened.

"Why?"

Cahill glanced at Lila before he answered.

"There's a posse being formed in town," he said briefly.

"Y'mean they're comin' after us again?"

The stocky man nodded.

"Yes."

Lila stepped forward.

"Is this some more of my father's doings?" she asked.

"We-ll," Cahill said. "I suppose you might say it is, particularly since he's leading the posse."

Curly grunted, wheeled and vaulted into the saddle.

"Wait!" Lila cried. She whirled, flashed over the ground to his horse, gripped the bridle. "Curly, take me with you, please! If anything's going to happen to you, I want it to happen to me, too!"

Cahill blinked. He coughed behind his hand but neither Lila nor Curly paid any attention to him now.

"No, honey," Curly said, shaking his head. "It wouldn't be right. You might get hurt an' I'd never f'rgive myself."

Lila stiffened.

"Curly Walker," she said severely. "Will you take me with you, or shall I find my way to your place by myself?"

The youth turned and looked in Cahill's direction. Cahill hastily looked away.

"We-ll?" he heard the girl demand impatiently. "We're wasting valuable time here, you know."

"Golly, Lila," Curly said protestingly. "You know I'd do anything f'r you but—"

"Would you?" she retorted.

" 'Course I would."

"All right. Then give me a hand up."

Cahill stole a quick look. He saw Curly bend down, throw his left arm around Lila's waist. Almost effortlessly he swung her up on the saddle behind him. Curly's horse whinnied, and loped away. They were some fifty feet away when Curly pulled up, wheeled his mount.

"Thanks!" he yelled.

Cahill answered with a wave of his hand. For a minute after they rode away he sat motionlessly, then suddenly, he slapped his horse across the rump.

"Get going!" he yelled.

The surprised horse jogged off. Cahill promptly whacked him a second time, a ringing slap that sent him bounding away in pursuit. Cahill clung desperately to the reins as his mount pounded away. Presently, when he dared look up again, he found himself hardly more than twenty feet behind Curly. Again he whacked his horse; the animal snorted protestingly, wheezed and bolted away like a runaway. They tore past Lila and Curly, who turned their heads as Cahill came abreast of them and looked at him wonderingly, then he was past them. Cahill spurred his mount, and narrowed the distance between them. They started down hill presently and Cahill managed somehow to check his horse's pace. Fortunately the borrowed horse was winded; he offered no objection to a trotting gait. Minutes later, with Cahill still in the lead, they came in view of the house.

"Hey!" someone yelled from the doorway of the barn.

Cahill jerked his mount to an abrupt stop.

Tad Cole, a rifle in his hands, looked up at him for a moment, then he laughed.

"Shorty!" he yelled. "What'n thunder are you doin' 'round these parts?"

Both turned in the direction of the house when they heard the back door open. Eve came out. Just then Curly and Lila rode up. Cahill watched interestedly. Tad looked hard at them; Eve came forward quickly. Curly reined in, grinned a bit awkwardly.

"Tad," he called. "Be a good feller, will you, and give Lila a hand."

"Sure," Tad answered.

He strode up, remembered the rifle; he stopped, propped it up against the barn wall, then he trudged on. He looked up at Lila. She flushed beneath his gaze, but when he raised his hands to her, she turned to him and slid down. He caught her under the arms, lifted her out of the saddle and set her down on the ground.

"Thank you," Lila said.

Tad touched the brim of his hat in answer. Curly dismounted as Eve came up to him. Lila turned and the girls' eyes met.

"Hello," Eve said brightly, flashing a smile.

"Eve," Curly said quickly. "This is Lila. Lila, this is my sister, Eve."

"I think you'd better tell your sister the rest of my name," Lila said quietly.

"Now, look," Curly said. He turned resolutely. "Eve, Lila's father is Ben Priddy. That make 'ny diff'rence t' you?"

"Should it?" Eve asked.

Curly wheeled.

"There y'are," he said to Lila. "We know you ain't responsible f'r the things your father does."

Eve pushed past Curly.

"We're glad to have you here, Lila," she said simply.

"Thank you."

"Won't you—won't you come into the house?" Eve asked.

She did not wait for Lila to answer. She took the younger girl by the arm and they went into the house. Cahill had dismounted. He came around the horses and nudged Tad.

"If you can spare the time," he said. Tad turned to him.

"Oh, yeah, Shorty," he said. "Reckon I musta f'rgot about you f'r the minute. What brings you all th' way out here?"

Cahill frowned.

"This isn't a pleasure trip, I assure you," he said sharply. "Any travel that revolves around my riding a horse becomes very annoying."

Tad grinned at him.

"Yeah," he said with a brief glance at Cahill's mount. "That cayuse you're ridin' looks like he'd be anything but comf'table once you get aboard 'im."

"I don't believe I'll be able to sit properly or otherwise for a week," the stocky man said. "I rode this way to warn you and your friends of something I overheard in town this afternoon."

"Oh!" Tad said quickly.

"The sheriff and our friend, Ben Priddy, were rounding up a posse. I thought you'd be interested in that piece of news; hence my delightful ride."

"So Priddy hasn't enough yet," Tad mused.

"Evidently not. And if I might venture an opinion," Cahill continued, "I really think he means business tonight."

"He'll catch penty o' hell if he comes around here," Tad retorted.

"His men caught quite a lot of it the other night, too," Cahill pointed out. "Yet he's coming back for more. Can you and the Walkers, with even fewer men than you had then, hope to stand them off again and still emerge from such an attack alive?"

Tad frowned. He did not answer because he could not.

"There's something else for you to consider," Cahill went on. He nodded toward the house.

"Y'mean the girls?"

"Of course."

"Look," Tad said. "Dan Walker's out in the fields. Come on. We'll go see him. This is his place now, y'know, so it's up t' him t' decide what's t' be done."

Cahill considered the suggestion for a moment, then he shook his head.

"Do you mind very much," he asked, "if I stay right here?"

Tad grinned at him.

"Y'mean your backside hurts too much t' walk?"

"In other words."

Tad hitched up his pants.

"You stay put here till I get back," he said. "I won't be long."

"I'll wait."

Tad looked at Curly; the youth had been standing there quietly, simply listening and offering no opinion.

"Curly," he said. "You keep Shorty comp'ny f'r a while, will you?"

"Sure thing."

"He talks kinda funny at times," Tad added with a wink, and Curly grinned. "Not like you an' me, still I suppose it's English, so do th' best you can with 'im. He ain't a bad sort."

He whacked the stocky man on the back and started away. He stopped suddenly, turned and retraced his steps.

"Hey," he said to Cahill. "It's gettin' late, y'know, an' maybe you oughta be gettin' back t' town b'fore one o' Priddy's hands gets wise t' what you've been up to. I don't want you gettin' into trouble with that polecat."

"We-ll—"

"Well, what?"

"I'm not much of a hand with a gun," Cahill said. "But I suppose, if the occasion demanded it, I could probably do all right with one."

Tad eyed him.

"What are you drivin' at?"

"I'd prefer to stay here, hang it," the little man exploded.

"O-h—I see."

"That's an improvement," Cahill retorted, and Curly laughed.

"Y'mean you're lookin' f'r an opportunity t' join your ancestors ahead o' time?" Tad demanded.

"I mean I'm looking for an opportunity to do something worth while with my worthless self for a change!" Cahill yelled. "Do I have to make it any plainer than that?"

"Nope," Tad replied, and then he laughed. "You're awright, Shorty. An' unless I miss my guess it'll be awright f'r you to figger on stayin' put here. I'll tell Dan he's got 'imself another hand."

Dan Walker, his rifle over his shoulder, was trudging toward the house when he spied Tad striding in his direction. He looked up questioningly, quickened his pace.

"S'matter?" he called when he was about twenty feet away. "Somethin' wrong?"

"Got somethin' to talk t' you about," Tad answered.

"Oh!" Dan said.

They faced each other presently.

"What's botherin' you?" Dan asked. "It must be somethin' that couldn't keep or you wouldn't've hot-footed it out here."

"Fellow I know fr'm Shorthorn," Tad explained. "He's at the house now. Anyway, he came t' tip us off that Priddy and the sheriff are roundin' up a posse."

"I see. An' what does this feller figger our comp'ny oughta be showin' up?"

"T'night."

"Soon as that, eh?"

"Yep. And Cahill, the feller I've been talkin' about, set me to thinkin' with somethin' else he said. He wanted t' know what we were gonna do. An' the more I think about it, the less we actu'lly c'n do. Figger it out y'self. Clark's gone, Eddie's gone, Walt's gone, and so is your Dad. Only thing we've still got the same is the girls."

"Girls?" Dan repeated. "There's on'y Eve now. You f'rgettin' that Doreen's gone?"

"Nope. But I was forgettin' something else. I forgot that you didn't know about Curly bringin' his girl home. She and Eve make two."

"Wait a minute," Dan commanded. "Don't go so fast. What's this about a girl?"

"Her name's Lila, and b'lieve me, that brother o' yours knows how to pick 'em!"

"You say her name was Lila?" Dan asked. "Never heard o' her. What's more, I didn't even know Curly had a girl."

"We-ll, you know now."

"I'll be that's why he's been moonin' around so quietlike."

" 'Course," Tad said. "An' you c'n make another bet while you're at it that it was on accoun' o' her that he wouldn't go back with Doreen."

"That's right. Who is this Lila?"

Tad grinned at him.

"How's your heart, Dan? Can you take it?"

"Try me."

"Awright, I will. Lila's full name is Lila Priddy."

Dan's eyes widened.

"Y'mean she's Ben Priddy's kid?"

"Yep."

"I'll be damned!" Dan said and then he chuckled. Tad eyed him. "If that don't beat all. Out of all the girls in this ornery world, he has t' go an' fall f'r the daughter o' the polecat who's been doin' everything he can t' hang him. It don't make sense t' me, but maybe it ain't supposed to."

"Gettin' back to other things," Tad said. "What do you plan t' do about Priddy and his posse?"

"What is there t' do but fight 'em? After all, Tad, this is home t' us, and we just can't pull out of it, y'know."

"You're the boss, Dan. But I just wanna point out t' you that it's gonna be tougher'n hell f'r us. There's you and me and Curly. That makes three. O-h, yeah, Cahill's throwin' in with us if it's awright with you."

"You know him, Tad. I don't."

"An' I don't know such a heck uva lot about 'im, either. I will say, though, that he seems t' be awright. 'Course I don't know how much good he c'n do us if it comes to a showdown, but he's willin' and that's somethin'."

"What've we got t' lose by lettin' him stay?"

"Nothing."

"Then tell 'im it's awright with me."

"Swell. Now, gettin' back again. There's the three of us, four countin' Cahill, and the two girls."

"Yeah," Dan said thoughtfully. "And if Priddy is really bent on wipin' us out, he shouldn't have too much trouble doin' it. Maybe we'd better pull out after all, huh? 'Course we c'n always come back when things quiet down again."

"That's what I was thinkin'."

Dan unslung his rifle, swung it under his arm.

"Come on then," he said. "It's gettin' later by the minute an' we've got things t' do if we're gonna pull outta here while we're still alive."

Side by side they strode back. There was no further conversation, for each was busy with his own thoughts. When they neared the barn, they looked up.

"That Cahill?" Dan asked. "The feller talkin' with Curly?"

"That's him awright. I don't know what his first name is. Fact is, Dan, I've never asked him. I call him Shorty, and he answers to it."

They heard a clatter of hoofs, turned and saw a woman astride a fleet-footed horse whirl up to the house.

"Hey," Dan said. "Who d'you suppose that is?"

"Don't ask me," Tad responded. "You sure she ain't the secret love o' your life? No tellin' with you Walkers, y'know."

When Dan quickened his stride, Tad followed suit. They saw Curly step around Cahill, saw him trot toward the house.

"I gotta find out what's goin' on around here," Dan said.

"Go ahead."

Dan swerved away from him, dashed after Curly. Tad continued toward the barn, trudged up as Cahill turned.

Dan says you can stay put here," he said.

"Thanks. And what does he propose to do about his visitors tonight?"

"We're pullin' out."

"Then he accepted your suggestion."

"Y'mean he accepted your s'ggestion. You gave me the idea an' I just passed it on t' him. Anyway, we're gonna hightail it but we're comin' back when things quiet down."

"Of course."

"If we still hafta fight, at least we'll be able to pick the spot an' that's a heap better'n havin' t' fight fr'm inside a house an' no chance o' gettin' out of it when the goin' gets tough."

Tad glanced toward the house. The horse on which the woman had ridden up was idling at the back door. The woman, Curly and Dan were nowhere in sight.

"Wonder where they went?" Tad asked.

"Obviously inside," Cahill answered.

The door opened and Dan came out. He shook his head, looked up, and when he found Tad and Cahill eyeing him, he grinned at them and came striding toward them.

"Well?" Tad demanded. "Who is she?"

"You won't b'lieve it when I tell you," Dan answered. He nodded to Cahill. "This ain't Mister Priddy's day."

"What's that supposed to mean?" Tad asked.

"Things are b'ginnin' to catch up with him," Dan said. "That was Missus Priddy."

"Huh? His wife? What's she want?"

"We-ll," Dan began. "Seems like it was this way. One o' Priddy's punchers didn't feel so good in town an' Ben got fed up hearin' him complain, so he sent him home. This feller came to the house and asked Mrs. Priddy for some medicine or somethin'. They got talkin' an' first thing y'know he f'rgot himself an' spilled the beans about what Papa Priddy was plannin' t' do t'night. Seems like Mama Priddy knew what was what b'tween Lila and Curly, so she figgered someb'dy better get word o' the raid to us. She hunted around f'r Lila an' when she couldn't find her, she came herself."

"Priddy'll be fit t' be tied when he hears about this," Tad remarked.

"Won't he though!"

"So his whole family's ganged up on him," Tad mused. "Looks t' me like Mister Ben Priddy's gonna be the man who walks alone!"

CHAPTER TEN

It was night, a dark, obscuring night filled with distorted and fantastically formed and quick darting shadows that frightened the uneasy and annoyed the rash who found it impossible to distinguish between and identify fitting forms and figures that looked man-made and man-like and which turned out to be something else again. The night sky was empty, and save for a dimmed light somewhere distant along the vast horizon, it offered little to probing eyes. It was a night that was made to order for those who needed darkness, obscuring darkness with which to cloak themselves and make possible the withdrawal they planned. A chilling wind arose with the advent of night and now it was cold; it rustled the leaves and grass, caught up dried, vagrant, curled-up leaves and dust and swirled them about noisily and aimlessly, then swerving, cast them aside. The darting wind, particularly when it burst through the leaves, seemed to murmur with an almost human voice, and that too was a bit disconcerting. But presently it was gone and the deepening silence was resumed.

There were three men idling near the back door. Their horses, long since saddled and brought out of the barn, waited a dozen feet beyond them. There was a second group of horses close by, too—Mrs. Priddy's, Eve's, Curly's gelding, and a fourth one, which showed its indignation at having been relegated to packhorse status by raising its head every now and then and voicing a disturbing, nasally whinnied protest. Each time, Dan turned his head and glared at the animal. Finally, when the horse's pained wailing reached a new high, Dan trudged over.

"Awright now," he said. "That's enough, so pipe down."

The horse, thinking he had gained a sympathizer, and misunderstanding Dan's words completely, gave his all in a final whinny. Dan's uncompromising hand rose and fell in a loud whack on the animal's rump.

"Now shut up," Dan said.

He started away, stopped and looked back over his shoulder; the horse, nursing a double hurt now, took both to heart for silent meditation, but wisely he refrained from making any further audible lamentations."

"We oughta get goin'," Tad said. "What's holdin' us up?"

"O-h," Dan said disgustedly. "Did you ever hear s'me women tryin' t' settle something? They've been at it f'r more'n an hour now. If they don't come outta there pronto, I'm goin' in an' haul 'em out."

"What's the argument about?" Tad asked.

"Mama Priddy wants t' head back home, while Lila wants t' stay here."

"Oh," Tad said. "Curly leave the barn doors wide open?"

"Yeah, sure," Dan answered.

Tad had suggested that the barn doors be left open, and the house be left in darkness. He argued that Priddy's raiders, if they found the barn open to their inspection, would leave it untouched, and he pointed out that a light in the house would invite a shattering blast of gunfire, whereas darkness and an unlocked door might arouse Priddy's suspicions. They would be allayed once he found it possible to enter the house and discover for himself that it had been abandoned. Of course, Tad had added, Priddy would be beside himself when he found that his quarries had fled; he would probably give vent to his anger by smashing things up a bit, but the house itself would doubtless remain untouched. Dan had listened to Tad's ideas attentively;

and he accepted them without modification when Cahill, who had little to say, nodded in agreement.

Curly came out of the house and the three men looked up.

"Well?" Dan demanded.

Curly sauntered over to them.

"They're comin' out," he announced.

"Argument settled?" Dan asked.

"Yep," Curly answered. "They're goin' t' Lee Pierce's place for the night, then in the mornin' Mrs. Priddy's goin' home."

"What about Lila?"

Curly shook his head.

"She's gonna stay with the Pierces."

"Where's their place?"

"I know where it is," Cahill said briefly.

Tad nudged Dan.

"Might be a good idea," he said, "if Cahill's willing, for him t' take th'm over there, then he could double back and meet us."

"Yeah," Dan said. "Be kinda foolish f'r any uv us, 'specially Curly, to do it. 'Course, it's like you said, Tad, if Cahill's willing."

" 'Course he is," Tad said. "He's had plenty o' time t' rest his fanny, so he won't mind herdin' the Priddy women folks over to the Pierces'. We'll hafta warn Lila an' her Ma that he's somethin' of a wolf with women, but b'tween them they oughta be able t' keep him in his place. I know Cahill, and I'll bet I know what he's figgerin'. Papa Priddy's luck is bound to run out one o' these days, and Shorty figgers this is a good chance f'r him and Mama to get acquainted so that when Ben cashes in his chips, Shorty'll be head man."

Cahill snorted loudly.

"Y'know," Tad continued, nudging Dan again. "Back home there was a feller named Trucks. He went f'r widows in a big way. Soon's he heard about a new widow, he hotfooted it over t' see her. He was the courtinest feller I ever heard of."

"What happened to 'im?" Dan asked.

"B'lieve it or not, he was courtin' six of th'm all at the same time. The one he finally got hitched to turned out t' be the worst bargain of th'm all. Y'see, Trucks didn't have any dough, an' this widow didn't have any either, an' the two o' th'm let on they had a-plenty. Into th' bargain, she had four kids, so Trucks, who wasn't one f'r workin', had t' go and find himself a job t' support th'm."

"That, my friend," Cahill said, "sounds very much like a hastily concocted yarn with absolutely no basis of truth."

"We-ll," Tad admitted. "Maybe I did lay it on a little here and there, but Trucks was the feller's name awright, and he did marry a widow."

"And the children?" Cahill pressed him.

"O-h, she had four like I said. What I f'rgot to mention was that Trucks had two o' his own."

"I shall be glad to escort the ladies to the Pierce place," Cahill said with finality.

"Thanks," Dan said.

The back door opened and Lila and her mother appeared in the doorway. The kitchen light went out. Mrs. Priddy stepped outside, then Lila, and then Eve, who drew the door shut behind her.

"Let's go," Dan said. "Curly, help Lila up. Tad, give Mrs. Priddy a hand like a good feller."

The Priddys were quickly mounted. Cahill climbed up on his horse, wheeled the animal, then he twisted around in the saddle and waited. Dan strode over to him, talked with him briefly. When he finished, Cahill nodded and Dan stepped back.

"Come, Lila," Mrs. Priddy said. She settled herself in the saddle, rode over to where Cahill was waiting. "Come, dear."

Curly reached up, drew Lila's head down; he kissed her soundly, grinned and stepped back. Lila straightened up, wheeled and guided her mount away. Cahill jogged off; the Priddys, the mother followed by her daughter, rode after him. They clattered past the barn as the others watched, and presently the night swallowed them up. For a brief moment there was a faint echo of hoofbeats, then it faded out completely.

"Awright," Dan said. "C'mon, Eve."

He followed her to her horse, helped her mount, then he strode over to his own horse, climbed into the saddle. Tad and Curly had already mounted. Curly leading the pack horse by a line which he had looped around his saddle horn, pulled the rope and drew the heavily laden animal closer to him, took another loop in the rope.

"All set?" Dan asked.

"Yep," Tad answered.

Dan whacked his mount with his open hand and the animal snorted protestingly and bounded away. Eve flicked the ends of her reins over her horse's head and he darted off. Tad, with Mike eager to run, followed close behind Eve. He turned once or twice to look back at Curly to make certain that the youngest Walker was having no difficulty with the pack horse. They rode eastward, strung out in a single line. Tad saw Eve turn her head for a last look at the house. Minutes later the wooded section loomed up in the distorting night light. When they neared the shadowy trees, Dan checked his horse's pace, held him to a jog until Eve and the others rode up.

"Watch it here!" Dan called. "Eve, you stick close t' me. Tad, you keep 'n eye on Curly!"

"Go 'head! You're holdin' up the p'rade!" Tad said.

Dan and Eve rode into the woodland, then Tad, with Curly at his horse's heels, followed.

It was almost midnight when a troop of eleven men riding in single file, with Ben Priddy in the lead and Sheriff Blix Higgins behind him, swung southward in the general direction of the Walker place. There was no talk among the riders. When one of their horses swerved off the cushioning grass and onto hard ground on which ironshod hoofs echoed metallically, Priddy promptly twisted around and glared at the offender.

"Watch it," he growled. "Don't hafta let them stinkin' home-steaders know ahead o' time that we're comin', y'know."

The errant horse was instantly jerked back into line. Higgins lashed his mount, overtook Priddy's, and pulled up alongside of him.

"What d' we do when we get there?" Blix asked. "Just surround th' place an' then rush it?"

"Yes," Ben replied. "But this time there'll be no holdin' back or pullin' back. We're gonna clean th'm out once an' f'r all, an' when we leave there, we're gonna know that th' Walkers just ain't 'nymore."

"Uh-huh," Blix said.

"Hold your place," Priddy ordered and the sheriff dropped back behind him.

It was probably twenty minutes later when they neared a wall of wild brush that Ben reined in.

"Pull up," he called over his shoulder. The horsemen behind him checked their mounts. "Awright, this is it. Get down."

The men dismounted, led their horses forward, tethered them behind the brush. Those who had rifles jerked them out of their saddle sheaths, slung them under their arms.

"Awright," Priddy called again, and they gathered around him. "We're goin' in. Blix, you take four men, and sneak in t' the left. The others'll come with me t' the right. Keep down low so's nob'dy c'n see you, an' watch where you're goin'. An' r'member, them damned homesteaders c'n shoot, so if you fellers aim t' come outta this alive, be careful. I don't want any o' you t' shoot till I give the word. But once we start shootin', don't stop shootin'. What's more, keep movin' ahead all th' time. That clear?"

There was a general nodding of heads and Higgins himself added a "Yeah, sure, Ben."

"One thing more," Priddy said. "If anybody has th' hard luck t' get hit, I don't want the feller nearest him t' stop an' take care o' him. We'll take care o' everything once it's over. That understood?"

"Yep," the sheriff said.

"Shut up f'r once, Blix," Ben said curtly, "an' give someb'dy else a chance t' say 'yes' or 'no' or whatever they wanna say. Awright, let's get movin'. Four o' you men foller Higgins. You other fellers foller me."

Four men, two of them armed with rifles, fell in behind Sheriff Higgins, who jerked out his Colt and trudged forward. The other men, one of them carrying a rifle, followed at Ben Priddy's heels. Quietly, some of them treading on tiptoe, the raiders pushed forward. Fifty feet from the barn Higgins' men swung away. Priddy led his group toward the barn, halted them in front of it. A stocky man with bandy legs—Joe Riggs, Priddy's foreman—nudged Ben.

"Doors are wide open, Boss," Riggs whispered.

"Yeah," Priddy replied. "Kinda funny."

"What d'you say I have a look inside?"

"Awright," Ben answered in a low tone. "On'y watch y'self. This may be a trick, y'know; them homesteaders are full o' th'm."

"I know a couple m'self," the foreman said with a sly grin.

He slipped past Priddy, made his way to the doorway and peered in; then he stepped into the building and presently disappeared in the darkness. A minute later he reappeared, came striding out.

"Empty," he announced.

"O-h, yeah?"

"Boss," Riggs said. "You don't suppose them mangy critters've handed us th' slip or somethin', do you?"

"We'll find out pronto," Priddy said. "Come on, you fellers. Foller me. We'll Work our way past the barn to the house. An' watch your step!"

In single file again, and with a scowling Ben Priddy in the lead, they made their way past the barn, hugging the towering, shadowy walls to avoid detection by probing eyes within the house. When they were clear of the barn, Riggs crowded up to his employer again.

"House is dark, too," Joe whispered. "What d'you make uv it?"

Priddy was grim-faced now. It had already begun to dawn on him that something had misfired. The wide-open barn doors and the dark house could mean but one of two things, and one of them he was quite ready to rule out. The remaining thing meant simply that the Walkers had slipped away in time to avoid annihilation. Priddy looked back at the men behind him; no, he told himself, they couldn't have forewarned the Walkers. He was equally certain that Blix Higgins and his men hadn't betrayed him. Doggedly, he went through with his "raid."

"We'll see what's doin' inside," he said to Riggs. "Take a couple o' men with you an' go in."

"Sure," Joe responded. "Here, you fellers. Two o' you foller me."

Riggs and the two men nearest him strode up to the house, tried the door, found it unlocked and stepped inside. There was a minute's wait, then a lamp flared and flamed into light in the kitchen. Presently, too, Riggs appeared in the doorway.

"They're gone, awright," he announced.

Priddy pushed past him into the house. The door slammed when Riggs followed him in; a few minutes passed, then the men still waiting outside heard a crash of dishes, a chair being hurled against a mirror. Then there was a sound of booted feet, and Priddy and Riggs and the other two men emerged from the house. Blix Higgins came panting up.

"What's up, Ben?" he gasped.

"They've gone," Priddy answered curtly.

"No kiddin'?"

Priddy pushed past him into the house. The door when Riggs followed him in; a few minutes passed, then the men still waiting outside heard a crash of dishes, a chair being hurled against a mirror. Then there was a sound of booted feet, and Priddy and Riggs and the other two men emerged from the house. Blix Higgins came panting up.

"What's up, Ben?" he gasped.

"They've gone," Priddy answered curtly.

"No kiddin'?"

Priddy turned away.

"Y'mean they found out we were comin'?" Higgins asked Riggs, stopping the man as he started to follow his employer away.

Joe shrugged his broad shoulder.

"I dunno," he replied. "All I know is that the barn's empty, the back door t' the house open, an' nob'dy's home. What d'you make uv it?"

Higgins drew in his breath with a curious, whistling sound.

"Hey!" he said excitedly. "I wonder if they could've been tipped off?"

"It sure looks a lot like it, don't it?"

"Don't it though!"

Riggs hitched up his belt.

"I'd sure hate t' be the feller who did it," he said grimly.

"Me too!"

They turned away from the house, trooped off in the darkness. Minutes later they reached the brush. They found Priddy already astride his horse. Higgins' four men appeared. They asked no questions; it was all too obvious to them that Priddy's plans had gone astray. Quickly they mounted their horses.

"Awright, Joe," Priddy called as he wheeled his horse.

Riggs guided his mount away from the others, clattered away after Ben. There were two of Priddy's punchers in the posse, and they spurred their horses and dashed after them. Higgins climbed into the saddle.

"Come on, fellers," he said. "We might's well get back t' town. I c'n do with a good, stiff drink, an' I know you c'n, too. Come on. The drinks'll be on me."

Priddy was surprised to find his house in total darkness when he rode up to it. He reined in, swung himself out of the saddle, handed the reins to Riggs.

"G'night, Boss," the foreman called as he and the two punchers clattered away toward the corral.

"G'night," Ben answered.

He looked up at the house. The frown on his face was deepening. Martha always left a light burning in the kitchen when she turned in and he was still away. He wondered about it as he trudged around the house to the rear. The back door was unlocked and he stepped inside, closed the door quietly behind him. He made his way to the table, fumbled in his pocket for a match, found one and struck it. Yellow light flared and sputtered, then the wick in the lamp flamed brightly. He picked up the lamp, went upstairs. Lila's door was ajar and he pushed it open wide, held the lamp aloft—her bed was untouched. He turned away and opened the door opposite. It was the room Martha and he had shared for the full twenty-seven years of their married life. The bed was untouched; the room was as completely orderly as always.

Slowly he tramped downstairs. The wooden steps creaked beneath him and he was surprised for he had never noticed that before. On the landing the piece of carpeting that always seemed to have one purpose in life, and that was to skid as he stepped on it, lay very, very still. He eyed it expectantly, but he managed to negotiate its length without any undue difficulty, trudged the length of the hallway, retracing his steps to the kitchen. He put the lamp on the table. He was tired, he suddenly realized, and he was hungry, too. He lifted the coffee pot, hefted it; he always did that, but it was different now, for the pot was empty. Slowly, almost incredulously, he put it down again. Usually, in fact nearly always, the pot was kept half filled, so that whenever he wanted a cupful, it took but a minute or two to warm it up. He couldn't recall when he had found the pot empty before. It was one of the many little things that had become so important in his life—and now the chain was broken. He took off his hat, scaled it across the room. It caromed off the far wall, dropped into a nearby chair, slithered out, and off to the floor.

For a while his eyes ranged over the room. How cold and silent it was now, yet how much living that room had known. It was always bright and alive, filled with tempting fragrances or aromas, but now it was hushed and full of faint echoes that defied identification. He swung a chair around, and seated himself on it. He moved closer to the table so that he could rest his arms on it. He wasn't particularly worried about Martha's absence; rather, he was annoyed at the fact that she had simply gone off somewhere without so much as a word to him. Of course, and he admitted it now, he'd been pretty gruff with her that morning, and with Lila, too; still, that was no reason for her to be nasty in turn. After all, it was a man's privilege to explode every now and then—he had to. It was a sort of outlet for the pent-up emotions and annoyances and worries that the average man was burdened with. Of course, women couldn't understand those things; their lives began and ended in a limited sphere. Their problems—and he shook his head when he used the word—were so unimportant, there really wasn't any comparison. Smart women knew that and they suffered these outbursts in silence; some women took them to heart but after a while, when the charged atmosphere had cleared and there'd been time for a little cry, all they needed was a kind word, a smile and perhaps a kiss, and everything was just fine again.

He frowned when he thought of Lila. It was about time he took that young lady in hand. It was one thing for her mother to make excuses for her .... He knew they were just excuses and now, as he thought of them, they began to annoy him, too. The way she'd been mooning about of late, and now the knowledge that she'd been seeing that confounded Walker boy, we-ll, it was high time something was done about her.

She'd changed a lot in the last few years; for that matter, so had Martha. Lila had always been a warm, affectionate child; now, he couldn't remember the last time she'd kissed him. He knew she was still just as affectionate with Martha. It sort of left him out in the cold. Sometimes when he'd come into the house, he'd hear them talking excitedly and laughing; then, when he appeared, their talking and their laughter ceased abruptly. Lila would dash off—there was always something terribly important to be done upstairs, something that demanded her immediate attention. Martha was just as bad. She'd get terribly busy with something that seemed to have little or no importance to him, some polishing or cleaning or anything that claimed her complete attention. Oh, he'd noticed those things even though he hadn't said anything. They weren't fooling him any, even though they might think they were.

Then there was the matter of education. He hadn't had very much, while Martha had had a lot of it. In the beginning, when he'd used the wrong words or mispronounced them or slurred some others beyond recognition, and she'd laughed at him, he hadn't taken offense. In fact, he had even laughed with her. In the last few years there hadn't been much laughter between them. Sometimes they seemed like strangers. They had drifted apart and it was Lila who had caused it. She had taken his place with Martha. They lived in one word, and he lived in another. They understood each other in a way in which he was in capable of understanding; they liked the same things, such as books. How many times he had come upon them, stretched out comfortably on Martha's bed or on the grass, reading a book together, lost in their enjoyment and understanding of it. How many times he'd stopped and listened as they discussed it, talking

so earnestly about people who weren't at all real but who simply existed between the covers of the book. He didn't go in for
make believe—the characters in his life were real. And because of
them, life was hard, and one had to fight continually for survival.
Of course they couldn't understand the practical side of life, and
he was as thoroughly practical as anyone could be.

His thoughts shifted again. Someone had forewarned the
Walkers. He wished he knew who had betrayed him. Then suddenly he sat upright in his chair.

"By God," he said aloud, and he pounded his fist on the table.
"By God."

He got to his feet, slung the chair out of his way.

"What a fool I've been," he muttered angrily. "Course it was
one of th'm. It was Martha, I'll bet, but it mighta been th' young
one at that. But I know damn well it was one o' the two, and when
I know f'r sure . . . ."

His jaws closed before he finished the sentence. He picked up
the lamp a second time and carried it upstairs. He had solved the
mystery that had plagued him. But now there was a new one to
haunt him. How had his betrayer learned of the planned raid? He
was still scowling when he got into bed.

CHAPTER ELEVEN

It was nearly eight o'clock the next morning when Martha Priddy dismounted at her own back door. She opened it, peered in, then she stepped inside, closed the door quickly behind her. Her eyes ranged over the room. She spied Ben's hat lying on the floor, and the overturned chair that he had angrily slung aside. She strode over, picked up the hat, lifted the chair and pushed it into place at the table, dropped the hat into still another chair, then she went upstairs. Lila's door was open and she glanced into her daughter's room as she passed it; her own door was open too and she stopped in the doorway briefly. The blinds were drawn. Ben's clothes were scattered about the room, with his shirt, pants and socks forming individual heaps on the floor. His underwear appeared to have been yanked off, turned inside out in the process of being removed, and then tossed aside. Then there were his boots—one lay on its side against the far wall, while its mate peered out from under the bed. Ben himself lay on his right side with his face to the wall and the blanket drawn up to his eyes.

Martha went to the window, raised the blind and flooded the room with sunlight, then she retraced her steps to the bed, and bent over her husband.

"Ben," she said.

There was no response.

"Ben," she said a second time. When he did not answer, she nudged him gently. "Ben."

He grunted, turned over on his back; he opened his eyes and blinked in the sunlight and quickly closed them again.

"Ben," she said for the fourth time and pushed his arm. "It's eight o'clock. You'd better get up."

He grunted.

"In a minute," he mumbled.

"Get up and get dressed," she said. "I'll have breakfast ready by the time you come downstairs."

"Awright."

She was halfway down the stairs when she heard him leap out of bed; she stopped and looked up. He was standing on the landing over her. She was tempted to laugh, for he made a ludicrous picture in his knee-long nightshirt. His hair was mussed and some of it stood up on end. He glowered at her through heavy-lidded eyes.

"So you're home, are you?"

"I got back a few minutes ago," she answered calmly.

"Uh-huh. Bein' that I'm your husband, I suppose it's awright f'r me t' ask where'n hell you've been, ain't it?"

"Of course," she said.

"Well?" he demanded.

"Oh!" she said, "I spent the night at the Pierces."

"You did, huh? Gettin' awf'lly chummy with that Ann, am'tcha?"

"I like Ann," she said evenly. "She's very real and down to earth when you get to know her."

"I see. How come you didn't tell me you were plannin' t' go see 'er?"

"You weren't here, so I couldn't very well tell you."

He scowled darkly, but she did not waver.

"Where's that daughter o' yourn?" he demanded. "That Miss High'n Mighty?"

"When I left the Pierces, Lila was still asleep."

"I dunno what's come over you o' late, Martha," he said. "But whatever it is, I don't like it."

"Could it be that the change you speak of is something you alone are responsible for?" she countered. "You aren't the man I married, Ben Priddy. You're someone else, a someone else I don't particularly like."

She turned and went downstairs.

Fifteen minutes later he came trudging into the kitchen. He sat down at the table. She brought him a cup of coffee, pushed the sugar bowl and pitcher of milk across the table; she turned away for a moment, then she placed a platter of hot biscuits in front of him.

"Where were you yesterday, Ben?" she asked.

"I was busy," he answered gruffly.

"So I assumed," she said quietly. "And what time did you come home?"

His head jerked upward and he glared at her.

"That's my business," he answered coldly.

"All right," she said calmly. "So it's your business. I happen to know where you were and what you were doing. The time you got home doesn't really matter."

He munched a biscuit, swallowed a mouthful of coffee.

"I'm awfully glad the raid didn't come off successfully," she said quietly, and he gulped. He put down his coffee cup, spilled some of the coffee on the tablecloth.

"Say that again," he commanded in a strange voice.

"I said I was glad the raid on the Walker place didn't come off successfully," she repeated.

He eyed her for a long moment.

"How did you know there was gonna be a raid?"

"O-h, I just knew. That's all."

He sprang to his feet, caught her by the wrist.

"I wanna know how you knew, y'hear?" he demanded. "An' you'd better talk an' talk fast."

"You're hurting me," she said.

His eyes narrowed.

"Talk," he commanded through his teeth and his grip tightened. "Talk!"

She twisted suddenly. Before he could throw up his free hand to defend himself, she struck him with a frying pan. He grunted, released her, staggered away; she gasped, dropped the pan and stared at him through wide, frightened eyes. He fell against the door. He shook his head to clear it; after a minute of tense silence, he straightened up, strode out of the room, trudged upstairs. A minute later he came down again. She heard the front door open and shut.

Curly Walker and Tad Cole had halted their horses atop a rise that gave them a view of the surrounding range. The morning sun was bright and warm and the range itself was alive with color and fragrance.

"Swell morning, awright," Tad said after a brief silence.

"Ain't it though!"

Tad eased himself in the saddle, hooked one long leg over the saddle horn.

"Curly," he said suddenly.

"Yeah?"

"Y'know, one o' these days you're gonna hafta do somethin' about clearin' y'self o' this Hassett business."

"I know."

"It was one thing b'fore you an' Lila met," Tad continued. "Now it's different. You've got y'self a girl now, an' a swell lookin' one, too, an' the first thing y'know, you kids are gonna wanna get married. But you know same's I do that you aren't gonna have a minute's peace till that business is cleared up."

"Tad, I know all that, b'lieve me. It—it keeps me awake at night, honest. But what c'n I do about it, huh? Tell me that."

"I dunno yet," Tad answered. "I'd hafta know th' hull story an' so far all I know is just that you were caught near th' Hassetts'

place, that you were charged with killin' th'm, an' that they were
all set t' string you up. Think you'd like t' fill in th' gaps so's the
thing'd make sense t' me?"

"Sure," Curly said quickly. "Where d'you want me to begin?"

Tad grinned at him.

"You might begin at the b'ginning," he said easily. "That's
allus th' best place when you're gonna tell a story."

"Awright," Curly said. "The Hassetts lived near th' creek. I'll
hafta ride over there with you one o' these days so's you c'n see
it f'r y'self. Anyway, Abe Hassett lived in a shack 'longside the
creek, while Judd, his brother y'know, had a place 'bout like Abe's
about a quarter uva mile away. Fr'm what I've heard tell o' th'm,
they lived there longer'n anybody c'n remember."

"What'd they do f'r a living?"

"Nobody knows f'r sure, Tad, 'cept they panned the creek,
fished, and managed somehow t' get along."

"Go on."

"I used t' go ridin' every day, and one day I found myself down
near the creek. Abe was pannin' the creek when I came along. He
went f'r his rifle right away but when he finished lookin' me over,
he kinda grunted an' put it down and went on with what he was
doin'. We got talkin' after a while, an' y'know, Tad, he wasn't a
bad sort at all. Pretty soon I started ridin' down an' stoppin' by
practic'lly ever day. He even got t' expect me."

Curly paused, moistened his lips with his tongue.

"He hated most everybody in Shorthorn," he went on again
shortly, "because everybody used t' laugh at him an' say he was
loco. He hated Ben Priddy an' Jess Vaughn more'n the others. I
think it was because he was afraid o' them that he hated th'm so
much. We-ll, one day when I was ridin' down toward the creek,
Ben and a couple o' his punchers come up on me suddenly, surrounded me. They wanted t' know what I was doin' down there,
an' more p'rticularly, what the Hassetts were doin'.'"

"What'd you tell 'em?"

"O-h, I gave th'm some kind o' answer an' Priddy told th'm to let me go. But that was only th' beginning. Fr'm then on I always saw somethin' o' Ben Priddy somewheres around the place. I told Abe about it an' somethin' happened to him. He got so danged excited, grabbed his rifle an' ordered me off the place. He kept hollerin' that I was in cahoots with Priddy, that Priddy'd sent me down there t' snoop around. Priddy, he hollered, was after his gold, an' I was bein' friends with him, Abe, y'know, just t' see if I could find out where he'd cached it."

"Go on, Curly. I'm listenin'."

"I stayed away f'r a couple o' days; then I rode down there again. Abe came bouncin' out fr'm behind some brush so sudden-like that he just about scared me an' my horse out of a year's growth. He made me turn around an' get outta there."

"Get down t' the last time."

"I'm comin' to it now," Curly said. "It was pretty late in the afternoon the last time I rode down tow'rd the creek. Y'know, Tad, I had the funniest feelin' inside o' me."

"Y'mean like you know somethin' was gonna happen?"

"Uh-huh. Even my horse started actin' up. He wouldn't stand still for a minute. He kept pawin' the ground, whinnyin' an' turnin' around all the time like he was expectin' somebody to pop up behind us. B'lieve me, I wish I'da got th' heck outta there right then 'stead o' hangin' around. Anyway, it got to be night, one o' those pitch black nights with no starts, no moon, no nothing. I could see somethin' uva light in the shack, then I kinda got the idea that I saw somethin' move just outside o' the shack. I went over t' see what it was."

"You were just beggin' f'r trouble, weren't you?"

"An' how, Tad. I heard a shot an' it seemed t' me that it came fr'm somewhere right near the shack, or maybe right inside uv it. I crept forward on my hands an' knees, but I couldn't see a danged thing. I got around to the front o' the shack an' then I saw that the door was open the tiniest little bit. I waited again but after a while, when nothing happened, I got the bright idea that maybe I oughta look in. I pushed the door open wider. Abe was sittin' at the table, sideways to the door, his left elbow on the table and his head restin' on his hand. Somethin' caught my eye right through the rungs o' the chair he was sittin' on. It was blood, and it was drippin' offa Abe to the floor. I jumped in, come around the table when he toppled outta the chair an' fell on the floor."

"What'd you do then?"

"O-h, I turned him over for one thing. There was a lotta blood on his head on the right side. That was where it was drippin' from."

"I see. Go on."

"I tried to lift him up, to get him back on the chair. Afterwards I realized that was kinda silly. Anyway, all uva sudden a couple o' men came rushin' in. We had one heck uva party. There was more fist swingin' th'n I've ever seen before, anywhere. Boy, I caught a couple o' wallops that were beauts. I musta passed out and when I came to, Ben Priddy was standin' over me, shakin' me. There was one feller I won't never forget. His name was Riggs, Joe Riggs. He's Priddy's forem'n. O-h, he f'r stringin' me up right then an' there. He called me th' dangedest names. An' then the sheriff came in. Ever seen him, Tad?"

"On'y in passing," Tad said with a grin. "He's big an' fat, ain't he?"

"He's big as a house. He came stridin' up t' me, wanted t' know what I did with the gold; told me murderin' the Hassetts was bad enough an' that I didn't hafta add robb'ry to my crimes. How d'you like that? It was all cut an' dried. I was there, so I was the murderer an' the robber t' boot. Someb'dy pushed me out, then a couple o' then got me up on my horse. I couldn't help myself. My hands were tied."

"Wait a minute now. You're gettin' too far ahead o' me. Didn't I hear someb'dy say in court that they found a lot o' things on you that someb'dy else said belonged to the Hassetts?"

"Uh-huh," Curly said, nodding. "All kinds o' little things. Junk. Th' sheriff found th'm on me when he searched me. But I give you my word, Tad, I never saw the danged things before that."

"Go on fr'm there."

"There was blood on me but I know I got that fr'm tryin' to lift Abe up. They made a lot outta that blood, b'lieve me. We started off f'r Shorthand. The sheriff rode alongside o' me an' kept talkin' t' me like a good feller. He wanted t' be my friend. All I had t' do was tell him where th' gold was."

"That's all, eh?"

"Uh-huh. O-h, here's somethin' I just remembered. They were all talkin' about two murders. I only heard one shot fired. My rifle was in my saddle boot, but later on the sheriff showed it t' me, an' I'm doggoned, Tad, if two shots hadn't been fired with it. I know I didn't fire 'em. I didn't even fire one shot."

"That the hull story?"

"Yeah, far's I c'n remember it now. Maybe I f'rfot some o' the little things, but they weren't important. If I think o' th'm later on, I'll make a point t' tell you about th'm."

"What about Mister Priddy? Didn't he have 'nything t' say t' you?"

"He saved his talkin' till we got t' the sheriff's office, then he told Sheriff Higgins t' leave us alone f'r a while. Boy, that fat Higgins moved. He's sure scared o' Ben Priddy."

"What did Priddy say t' you?"

"O-h, it was all about the Hassetts' gold. 'Course I didn't know where it was. I didn't even know f'r sure that they had 'ny. I told that to Priddy but he wouldn't hear uv it. He kept pressin' me to tell him an' I kept answerin' that I didn't know anything about it. W-hy, even if I did know, I'm danged if I'da told him anyway!"

"What'd he do when he couldn't get anything outta you?"

"O-h, he was mad awright. He fin'lly turned around an' went stormin' out."

Tad nodded understandingly.

"Now you know most everything that happened, Tad. What c'n I do?"

"Hey," Tad said quickly. "Don't go tryin' t' stampede me. You hafta gimme some time t' think about things. Meanwhile, we'd better head back for camp. Dan an' Eve'll start thinkin' things if we don't show up there pretty soon. Come on. Turn that horse o' yourn around."

They rode back to camp without further discussion.

The camp site Dan had chosen was high ground surrounded by huge boulders. It could be defended by a mere handful. The approach to the site was hard, pebbly ground and oncoming horses provided an alarm that could be heard for miles around. Dan was watching the approach from a boulder that commanded an unobstructed view, and when Tad and Curly appeared, he stepped out to meet them.

"Glad you fellers fin'lly got back," Dan said.

Tad looked at him quickly.

"S'matter?" he asked. "Somethin' happen?"

"Nope," Dan answered. "It's just that we've d'cided t' go back."

"That's awright with me," Tad said. "This campin' out ain't what it's cracked up t' be. It was awright when I was young...."

"An' now that you're beginnin' to feel your age," Dan said with a grin, "you're willin' to leave campin' out t' those who like it an' c'n take it."

"Right. When d'we start back?"

"Soon's you an' Curly are ready. Our stuffs packed."

"Everything I own's on me," Tad said. "How 'bout you, Curly?"

"I'm all set this minute."

"Swell," Dan said. "One o' you fellers take the pack horse. Eve, Cahill—come on. We're headin' home."

CHAPTER TWELVE

The deepening quiet of night was settling over the range when the furious pounding of hoofs broke the shadowy silence, and a lone horseman came into view. It was Tad Cole. He whirled Mike around a huge boulder, pulled her to a stiff-legged stop, and waited. Presently another horseman rode up, halted his mount momentarily while he looked about him, then he clattered past the boulder.

"Hey," Tad called, recognizing the man. Cahill pulled up, twisted around and looked at him. "An' where d'you think you're goin', huh?"

"With you," Cahill answered. "That's why I tried to overtake you."

"What was th' idea?"

Cahill smiled easily.

"You're up to something," he said calmly. "I could tell that by those supposedly innocent and casual questions you asked me this afternoon. And since I'm somewhat interested in the same matter, I decided to tag along with you. I know you won't object if I keep you company—or will you?"

Tad grinned at him, shook his head.

"No objections," he said. He wheeled Mike, gave her her head and she whinnied, trotted forward, ranged herself alongside Cahill's horse. "Go 'head, Shorty. Lead the way."

With Cahill in the lead, they rode eastward for a couple of miles, then Shorty pulled up, turned, waited for Tad to join him. Tad clattered up, looked at him questioningly.

"S'matter?" he asked. "What'd you stop for?"

"Consultation," Cahill replied. "What do you plan to do when you get there?"

"Dunno yet," Tad replied. "I figgered we might like to look around a little an' maybe we could kinda get n' idea fr'm what we see."

"All right."

"We near th' creek yet?"

"O-h, I don't think it's more than a quarter of a mile away."

"Then s'ppose we go on some more. 'Course we don't wanna ride right up t' the place. We c'n stop say a couple o' hundred feet b'fore we come to it, leave our horses an' go on fr'm there on foot."

"As you say."

It was dark now and they rode onward at a slower pace, with Mike clinging to the heels of Cahill's borrowed horse. Then they stopped a second time. They dismounted; there was a thicket a short distance away and Tad led Mike into it, tethered her there. Cahill came along directly, tied up his horse, too.

"See that shack down there?" Cahill asked.

Tad turned. His eyes followed his companion's pointing finger.

"Yeah, sure," he said.

"The creek's directly behind the shack," Cahill added. "It isn't very wide, probably less than twenty feet. If you look closely, you can see it from here. It's little more than a narrow silver ribbon. See it?"

"Nope," Tad answered. "O-h, yeah! I see it now."

"Now you take over," Cahill said. "What shall we do first?"

"I'd s'ggest that we have a close-up look at the shack," Tad said promptly. "We'll figger out the next thing afterwards."

They trudged off together. In the light night the shack loomed up dismally. They approached it from the rear, then circled around to the front door, halting there briefly while Tad's eyes ranged over the creek. The shack was less than fifteen feet upshore from the creek.

"Where's the other brother's place?" Tad asked in a low voice.

"Farther inland," Cahill answered in a guarded tone. "Something like half a mile straight north of here."

Tad's hand tightened around the door knob. Cahill nudged him.

"Careful," he whispered.

Tad nodded in reply. He turned the knob slowly. The door opened, creaked, and opened wider. Tad pushed Cahill away, then he jerked out his gun, waited, peering into the darkened shack.

"Oughta be a lamp somewheres around the place," he said finally. He stepped into the shack. A match flared suddenly and Cahill, standing in the doorway, saw Tad stride across the floor. A yellowish light flamed startlingly bright, then it was hastily turned down. "Awright, Shorty. You c'n come in."

Cahill crossed the threshold. He sniffed loudly.

"Stinks in here," Tad said. "Don't it?"

"Very much so."

There was a tattered blind drawn full over the single window. Cahill's eyes ranged over the shack. There was a table in the very middle of the room, a heavy, crude, makeshift affair; there were three chairs scattered around the room, and two of them had no backs. There was a bunk in the far corner; there was no bedding in it, nothing but a soiled blanket that lay in a limp heap at the foot of the bunk. Tad stepped around the table, and closed the door.

"Well?" Cahill asked. "What now, my young friend?"

Tad did not answer. Instead, he retraced his steps, knelt down beside the bunk, fumbled with the blanket and finally tossed it aside; then he bent lower, probed under the bunk. After a minute he got to his feet, looked at Cahill and shook his head. Cahill shrugged his shoulders. Tad picked up the lamp, carried it to the far corner, got down on his knees. Inch by inch he went over the floor while Cahill watched and waited. He covered the shack floor from corner to corner and wall to wall, then he got to his feet again, stiffly, put the lamp on the table. Cahill looked up at him.

"It ain't in here," Tad said.

"Finding the Hassett gold in here would have been far too easy," Cahill remarked. "Depend upon it, Tad, this place has been gone over time and again. Trust Priddy for that."

"I know," Tad said. "I know."

Cahill stood by patiently, quietly; when Tad blew out the light, he simply trudged to the door, opened it, waited in the open doorway; then when Tad sauntered toward him, he stepped outside. Tad came out, closed the door behind him. For a few silent minutes he stood there, in the shadows thrown off by the shack. Cahill did not interrupt his thoughts.

"Shorty," he said suddenly.

"Yes?"

"Where'd they plant th'm?

"I beg your pardon?"

"The Hassetts," Tad said impatiently. "Where'd they bury th'm?"

"Oh!" Cahill said. "I don't know, Tad. However, it must be somewhere close by here. Why do you ask?"

"I was just wonderin'."

"What about?"

"Forget it."

"You've something in mind. What is it?"

"Y'mean you really wanna know?"

"N-o, but you're going to tell me eventually, so I suppose I might just as well know now."

Tad laughed shortly.

"I was wonderin' what the Hassetts would have to say if—"

"Dead men, you know, aren't supposed to tell tales or bear witness."

"I know. Maybe the Hassetts don't know that."

Cahill drew a deep breath.

"Go on," he commanded.

"You game, Shorty?"

"For what?"

"T' dig th'm up."

"I was afraid that was what you were planning to do."

"So now you know. Look, Shorty, f'r my money the only chance we've got o' gettin' anywheres in this mess is t' find somethin' that'll—"

"You mean a clue."

"Huh? Yeah, that's right—a clue. Priddy's smart enough t' leave nothing f'r anybody t' work on. Th' on'y thing he couldn't do 'nything with would be a dead man. That's why I'm stakin' everything on findin' somethin' on the Hassetts."

"H'm."

"Y'know, I had a talk with Curly this mornin'. Its doggoned tough on that kid, not bein' able to do 'nything to help himself in this murder business. Somebody else has got t' do it for him. What d'you say?"

"What can I say?" Cahill retorted. "I asked for this, didn't I? I insisted upon coming along with you, so I can't very well refuse whatever help I can give you."

"An' I suppose I oughta say, 'G'wan, Shorty. You hightail it. I c'n handle this by myself.'"

"But you're not saying it."

"Nope," Tad said calmly. "Two c'n do this job a heap better'n one, so I'm doggoned if I'm gonna let you get out've it. Think you c'n recognize the Hassetts if you see them again?"

"Unfortunately, yes."

"That's all I wanna know. Look, suppose you start scoutin' around f'r the graves while I go back inside an' get the shovels I saw layin' under the bunk?"

"You'd better bring that lamp, too. We'll need it, once we find the Hassetts."

"Right," Tad said and he turned away and trudged back into the shack. He reappeared a minute later with the shovels swung over his right shoulder, and the lamp gripped in his left hand. He heard a whistle and he stopped and looked up. "Doggone if he ain't found th'm already," he said admiringly.

He strode briskly toward Cahill.

"Here they are," the latter said.

"Gotta hand it to you, Shorty," Tad said. He put down the lamp, followed it with the shovels.

"It was purely accidental that I found the graves so quickly," Cahill said. "I tripped over the mound."

Tad grunted, rolled up his sleeves, picked up one of the shovels and started to spade down the mound. He worked quickly, easily. Cahill watched him for a minute.

"I suppose," he said, "I could be useful as well as ornamental."

"It's 'n idea," Tad said. "Know which end uva shovel t' use?"

Cahill did not answer. He picked up the second shovel and went to work. It was probably half an hour later when Tad stopped him.

"That's enough," he said. "I just hit somethin'."

He tossed his shovel aside, bent down.

"Good thing they didn't bury 'im too far down," he said. "Gimme a hand here, Shorty. You take his feet."

Cahill "took" the dead man's feet, helped Tad lift the corpse out of the shallow grave.

"Maybe we oughta lug him inside." Tad suggested. "Then we c'n look him over careful-like and without worryin' about anybody seein' lamp light."

Cahill did not reply; he was conserving his strength. They carried the dead body into the shack, laid it on the bunk.

"This gonna upset you?" Tad asked.

"I was a doctor," Cahill said. "It seems ages ago—still it's true. So perhaps you'd better let me do the probing."

"Swell," Tad said quickly. "I've seen dead men but this is a little diff'rent."

"You might bring that lamp in here," Cahill said. "Light it and set it up on the table. Then if you can find something that has a bottom to it, you can fill it with water from the creek. I can use some."

"Right."

Tad went striding out. He returned shortly, placed the lamp on the table, lit it, then he scoured the shack for a bucket, found one finally and went out with it swinging from his hand. It was minutes later when he came back.

"Where d'you want this?" he asked.

Cahill was bent over the figure on the bunk.

"On the table," he said over his shoulder. He came erect presently. He had a piece of cloth in this hand; he dipped it into the water, turned again and went back to the bunk. Tad waited patiently. "How were they supposed to have been killed?"

"They were s'pposed to've been shot," Tad answered. "Leastways, that's what I understood someb'dy to say."

"H-m."

"Find th' bullet wound?" Tad asked.

"Yes," Cahill replied. "Only it wasn't a fatal wound by any means. It was just a superficial wound. The bullet, as I figure it, grazed the right temple, stunned this man, and probably resulted in a great deal of bleeding. But it didn't kill him. Not by any stretch of the imagination."

"Then what did kill 'im?"

"That," Cahill said, "is what I am looking for. When I find out, I'll be glad to let you know. Turn up that lamp a bit, will you? I can use some more light now."

It was midnight when Tad and Cahill rode back to the Walker Place. They were unsaddling their horses when Tad turned to his companion.

"Mind my askin' you somethin'?"

"I've been wondering why you didn't ask it sooner," Cahill replied. "You didn't say a word on the ride back, and I assumed you were trying to frame your question properly, and that when you were ready, you'd ask it."

"Why'd you quit doctorin'?"

"Why?" Cahill repeated heavily. "I discovered too late that liquor and medicine don't mix very well. They're opposed to each other."

"Y'mean somethin' happened?"

"Yes."

"Oh." Tad said. "It must've been pretty bad, huh?"

"Very bad. I killed a man."

"Y'mean while you were—"

"Drunk? Yes. It was the simplest thing that I was doing: a simple incision that even the most incapable and inexperienced medical student could have performed and acquitted himself well. My hand was unsteady and I cut far too deep."

"That was sure tough."

"On both of us," Cahill said. "I walked out of my office and never returned to it. That was over ten years ago, in Kansas."

"But haven't there been times when you wanted t' get back into harness again an' do what you were trained t' do?"

"In the beginning of my exile, yes. Then as the years went by, I lost every desire, every hope. Actually, Tad, I lost myself. I made myself a nobody, did nothing, simply sank as low as it was possible for a human to sink. Now you know more about me than anyone else does."

"Nob'dy will ever hear it fr'm me," Tad said quickly. "You c'n bank on that."

"Thank you," Cahill said. "Now let me ask you something. What are you going to tell the Walkers?"

"Just that Curly's innocent o' what he's been charged with. I can't tell th'm any more till I know more. Come on, we'd better go in now. Eve's probably waitin' up, wonderin' and worryin' about us.

Eve Walker was sitting at the kitchen table, a sewing basket on her lap, when they entered the room. She turned quickly when the door opened.

"Oh," she said, and smiled. She put the basket on the table. "I'm glad you're back. I was just going to make some fresh coffee. You'll have some, won't you?"

"Sure," Tad answered.

Cahill shook his head.

"No, thank you," he said. "Coffee keeps me awake at night. So if you'll excuse me, I'll turn in."

"Of course," Eve said.

"Good night."

"Good night," Eve answered. Cahill went out of the room. They heard his door close shortly. "I like him, Tad. But he's a strange man, isn't he?"

"O-h, I dunno. He's learned a lot o' things—in college, y'know—an' he talks different th'n we do, that is, the way I do, but that's all. He's been pretty regular far's I'm c'ncerned. S-ay, where's Curly? And Dan? They gone to bed?"

"Dan's asleep. But Curly's still awake. He was thumbing through an old book. Want him?"

Tad nodded.

"Yep," he said. "Got some swell news f'r him."

Eve's eyes widened.

"Oh, Tad!" she said. She got to her feet. "I'll call him."

She raced out of the room. She returned presently followed by Curly.

"What's up?" he asked.

Just wanted you t' know that Cahill an' I did some checkin' up t'night," Tad answered. "We found out that you never killed the Hassetts."

" 'Course I didn't!" Curly said heatedly. "Thought you knew that."

"Wait a minute," Tad said quickly. "That wasn't what I meant t' say at all."

Curly glared at him. Eve came up beside him, slid her arm through his.

"What I meant t' say," Tad went on, "was that we c'n prove you didn't do it."

Curly's eyes softened. Eve smiled at him, tightened her hold on his arm.

"You say you an' Cahill c'n prove it?" Curly asked.

"Yep. But that ain't enough. We need a little more time t' pin the killings on the right party. Then you'll be free as the air. Nob'dy'll be able t' point a finger at you. That's all there is t' tell you up t' now."

Curly laughed emotionally, nervously.

"That's all, he says!" he said to Eve. "Gee, wati'll I tell that to Lila!"

"Look," Tad said. "When Priddy an' that fat sheriff o' his grabbed you, they accused you o' shootin' the Hassetts t' death, didn't they?"

"Uh-huh," Curly said, nodding.

"They even swore t' that in court, didn't they?"

"They sure did," Curly said. "But why are you harpin' on that f'r?"

Tad grinned at him knowingly.

"O-h, I just wanted t' know I'd really heard that, and that I just didn't dream it up. That's all. G'wan now—g'wan back t' your book."

"The heck with the book!" Curly said, and he laughed again. "I'm goin' to bed. For the first time since I c'n remember, least-ways it seems that long t' me, I'm gonna stretch out an' really do a job o' sleepin'. O-h, boy—I'm in the clear!"

He threw his arms around Eve, smothered her in a bear-like hug, kissed her soundly, then released her. He turned to Tad, held out his hand.

"Thanks, Tad," he said gravely. Their hands met, gripped. "Thanks a million."

"Forget it."

Curly turned and went out of the room. Eve and Tad did not move. They stood where they were and looked at each other, then Eve's head came down.

"S'matter?" he asked quickly.

"I-I'm going to cry."

"Hey," he said protestingly. "For Pete's sake!"

"I-I can't help it."

"Wa-al," he said, equally helplessly. "Awright then."

A sob escaped her. He reached out for her, gripped her shoulders; she came to him willingly, and he held her tight. Her tears dampened his shirt front. He bent his head a bit.

"Eve," he said gently. "Eve."

Her head was just below his lips now. There was no explaining what happened then. Actually, he relived the moment a hundred times after, but he never made any attempt to reason it out. There was no need for that. It was a moment he had never experienced before, and he was completely delighted with it. He buried his face in her hair, and then he kissed her. Her sobbing stopped instantly, miraculously. She raised her head. Their eyes met for a brief second, then her arms swept upward and tightened around his neck. His arms tightened around her fiercely. His lips found hers, crushed them, bruised them in a lingering kiss that left them breathless, and perhaps a little dazed. She broke away from him, backed off a step or two, wheeled suddenly and fled.

He stopped briefly in Cahill's room before he went on to his own room. Cahill was just dozing off. When he heard Tad's step he twisted around in bed.

"How—how was the coffee?" he asked drowsily.

"Huh? Coffee? What coffee?"

Cahill made a funny sound, then he dropped down again on his back. He drew up the covers, settled himself deeply, and sighed contentedly.

"G'night," he said, and turned over on his side.

Tad did not answer. His thoughts were elsewhere and Cahill's voice failed to reach him. But minutes later a wheezing choking snore jolted him back to reality, and he looked down at the offender in surprise.

"Huh?" he said. "O-h, g'night, Shorty."

He turned and went out, returned almost immediately to close Cahill's door, then he trudged into his own room. He closed the door behind him, groped his way in the darkness to the bureau, made a light in the lamp that stood on it. Slowly he unbuttoned his shirt, turned away, stopped when he caught a glimpse of himself in the mirror that hung above the bureau. For a full minute he peered at his reflection, studied it intently.... When he moved away toward the bed there was no indication of approval or disapproval. There was, however, a curious lightness in his head, and his lips burned and tingled strangely. He moistened his lips with his tongue; he raised his hand, touched his lips tenderly, looked at his fingers when he drew them away.

He undressed himself, although the next morning he couldn't remember it, got into bed, covered himself up, closed his eyes only to open them again a minute later—he had forgotten to blow out the light. He kicked off the covers and climbed out of bed, plodded across the room and blew out the light, groped his way back to bed, got in again, whipped up the covers. For a short time he lay flat on his back, then as sleep overcame him, he eased over on his side, and finally on his stomach. He sighed and grunted, made other indistinguishable sounds, then after a brief interlude of almost complete silence, he began to breathe deeply. He was asleep. Then Eve's face appeared in his dreams and his arms curled around his pillow.

CHAPTER THIRTEEN

The night sky was a bright, velvet-soft blue, moonlit and star-studded. The air was fresh and crisp, at times almost chilling. A breeze that danced lightly over the far-spreading range stiffened and became a wind that droned noisily over the flatland; when it reached the creek it swerved sharply, banked and raced away toward the south. Leaves and dust fluttered a bit after it had gone, then finally settled themselves and the range was hushed again.

Tad and Cahill rode slowly toward the shack. When Tad jerked Mike to a sudden stop, Cahill halted his horse, too, and was almost jolted out of the saddle.

"What is it?" he asked quickly.

"Sh-h!" Tad fairly hissed at him. "Not so loud. I got 'n idea we aren't the on'y ones here t'night. Kinda thought I saw a light in the shack."

Cahill turned instantly, frowned, focused his eyes on the shack a hundred feet ahead of them. Tad was motionless, rigid and tensed. He kept his eyes fixed on the shack's window.

"Well?" he said finally, out of the corner of his mouth. "See 'nything?"

"I think I did," Cahill said guardedly. "But I wouldn't want to swear to it. It may have been just my imagination."

Tad frowned, grunted something indistinct.

"Get down," he said shortly. "That thicket's somewheres off t' the right. We'll leave th' horses in there, then we'll go have a look at the shack fr'm up close. Climb down."

They dismounted, led their horses away. The thicket proved to be even closer at hand than they had expected it to be; they were within its protective shadows in a matter of minutes, then out of it, on foot, with Tad in the lead, and Cahill, a rifle clutched tightly in his somewhat clammy hands, following at Tad's heels. Swiftly they strode toward the shack. Cahill needed no instructions this time. He knew Tad would head for the rear of the structure for a peep into the window. If they had imagined it, and there was no light in the shack, then they would relax; if there was someone within the shack, we-ll, Tad would decide what was to be done. Cahill liked the youth, liked his breezy manner and his equally breezy insolence. At the same time, association with Tad had given Cahill confidence in him, and in his capabilities. Tad, he knew, always gave a good account of himself. Now, with Tad's tall, rangy figure directly ahead of him, swinging along with absolutely no thought of fear or hesitation, he suddenly felt that he too would have to be reckoned with if anything happened. He felt actually warlike, belligerent, and he found himself hoping that they would find someone in the shack. He saw himself matching strides with Tad, standing in a swirl of gun-smoke, blasting away with an air of abandon, plunging into an imaginary fray with a fury that left him a bit winded and breathless. He stumbled from his exertion and Tad stopped, whirled around and looked at him.

"Watch it," Tad said sharply.

Cahill did not answer; instead, he closed the gap between them. They went on again.

They were within a dozen feet of the shack when Tad stopped a second time, turned and reached out for him, caught him by the arm and brought him close.

"Someone's in there awright," Tad whispered in his ear. "See the pinpoints o' light through the window shade?"

Cahill raised his eyes; his heart began to pound like a trip-hammer.

"Yes," he whispered back. "Who—who d'you suppose it is?"

"Dunno."

"What'll we do?"

"I'm gonna sneak up t' the window for a look-see. You drop back an' kinda keep 'n eye on things in general. Get it?"

"Yes, of course."

Tad stepped past him, glided away. Cahill saw him reach the rear wall of the shack, saw him flatten out against it, then he saw Tad inch his way toward the window. He saw Tad crouch down a bit in front of the window. He started to drift away, as Tad had instructed, when the youth turned and motioned to him. Cahill's belligerency vanished. He gulped and swallowed, hesitated.... When Tad motioned to him again, he braced himself, gripped his rifle anew, and trudged forward. He crouched down beside Tad.

"What—what is it?" he asked in a strained whisper.

"Priddy's in there awright," Tad answered. "There are two others with 'im. I don't reco'nize th'm. See if you know th'm."

Cahill came erect. He moved over to the window. The worn shade fell to within an inch of the window sill, leaving him just enough room to peer into the shack. Presently he moved away from the window.

"Well?" Tad asked.

"One of them is Joe Riggs, Priddy's foreman. The other is one of Priddy's punchers—a fellow named Rock. What's it all about? They're just standing there, looking at each other."

"Dunno," Tad answered. "But I aim t' know an' pronto, too. Now look, Shorty. I'm goin' around t' the front. The door's open. Did you notice it?"

"No—I didn't."

"We-ll, it is. You stay here at the window. If I get into anything an' I need help, you c'n take a hand with your rifle. But don't you start pumpin' lead till I holler f'r you. Understand?"

He stepped around Cahill, slipped away. Cahill drew a deep breath, then he moved closer to the window and peered in.

Priddy was standing on one side of the table; Riggs and Rock were facing him. Cahill looked past them to the door. It was open just the barest bit.

"Wa-al, boss?" Cahill looked up quickly when he heard Riggs' voice. "We're gonna give you this last chance t' snap up our proposition. We know it was you who killed the Hassetts. We know you did it on accoun' o' their dough. But we ain't lawm'n, so the hell with the killin' part. It's the dough we're interested in. Split it three ways an' nob'dy'll ever know 'nymore about what happened t' the Hassetts than they do now. But if you're gonna be pigheaded about it, awright. You c'n take all th' dough and swing, or you c'n do business with us an come outta this with a good-sized hunk f'r y'self, and with a hull skin. Now what d'you say?"

"You're plumb loco, Joe," Priddy sputtered. "I didn't have 'nything t' do with them killin's. I don't need the Hassetts' dough. I got more'n enough o' my own."

"That ain't th' way I've heard it," Riggs retorted.

The man named Rock laughed.

"Everybody in town knows th' bank's holdin' enough o' your notes t' paper the walls o' the buildin'," he said scornfully. "So why don't you quit kiddin' us, huh?"

"Hold it, Rocky," Riggs said with a gesture. "Lemme do th' talkin'."

Rock turned away but he whirled around again.

"S'ppose you tell us what you were doin' here, huntin' around under th' bunk, when we barged in?" he demanded. "Huh?"

"I "I—I was lookin' f'r somethin'," Priddy answered.

"Yeah?" Rock retorted. "F'r what?"

"I was lookin' f'r somethin' that'd lead me to the killer," Priddy said doggedly. "Y'know—a clue."

Rock laughed again.

"G'wan," he said. "Y'know—a clue."

Rock laughed again.

"G'wan," he said. "Y'know, boss, I usta think you were a pretty smart feller. But you ain't, not by a jugful. You had things fixed up just right f'r that Walker kid t' swing f'r th' killin's. It was a natural. You had th' judge an' that Cummings feller on your side, witnesses, everything. Then you let 'n outsider spoil everything. You went after the homesteaders t' wipe th'm out. They outsmarted you, made a monkey outta you. Seems t' me, everything you touch you mess up. Now why don't you smarten up, huh, an' listen t' reason, b'fore you wind up at th' end uva rope?"

"We're wastin' a lot o' time gabbin' an' gettin' no-wheres," Riggs said curtly. "What's the answer, Priddy? Do we do business—or don't we?"

"Yeah," Rock added. "Talk up. If it's a deal, awright. If it ain't, it's awright too, and we'll go on our way. It's a long ride t' town, y'know, an' if we're goin', we wanna get started. An then more'n likely we'll have a helluva time rousin' th' sheriff when we do get there. That Higgins sleeps like a log once he hits the hay. An' if he's got 'ny liquor in 'im, it'll take a bunch o' whoopin' C'manches t' wake him."

"What d'you say, Ben?" Riggs asked.

"Doggone it, Joe," Priddy said, leaning forward on the table. "An' that goes f'r you too, Rocky. You fellers are barkin' up th' wrong tree. I didn't have a damned thing t'do with killin' the Hassetts."

"C'mon, Joe," Rocky said. "Let's get goin'."

He pushed past Riggs to the door, stopped and looked back over his shoulder.

"You comin'?" he asked.

"Wait a minute," Riggs answered without turning. "Ben, we've been t'gether a long time. I sure hate t' do 'nything to hurt you, but you're forcin' me to. Why don't you get wise t' y'self? 'Stead o' tryin' t' bluff us, come clean with us. Make us a proposition, will you?"

Priddy did not answer. He came slowly erect. Riggs waited briefly, then he shrugged his shoulder, turned on his heel and trudged to the door. Rock reached for the knob, gripped it, turned it. The door flew open.

"Reach!"

It was Tad's voice and Cahill's thumping heart stood still.

"Reach, I said!"

Rock seemed to hesitate for a moment, then his hands started upward, slowly, reluctantly. Joe Riggs who was slightly behind him, suddenly twisted away. His right arm jerked back and his hand streaked toward his holster. His gun flashed in his hand, snapped upward when a Colt thundered deafeningly from the doorway. The shack seemed to rise up off the ground, and the echo of the blast filled the limited space of the flimsy wooden structure. Then the shack seemed to settle down again, and the ear-splitting roar began to fade. Blue gunsmoke that had swirled around the doorway began to lift gently. Cahill's bulging eyes found Riggs; the man was standing midway between the table and the wall. He was clutching his right wrist and blood was seeping through the fingers of his left hand; Cahill's eyes followed it down, saw it drip noiselessly on his boots and on the floor. Riggs' gun, he noted, too, lay at his feet.

"You, Priddy," Cahill heard Tad say and his eyes shifted again. "Keep your hands where they are an' don't make 'ny moves. This trigger finger o' mine gets awf'lly itchy, y'know, an' it's liable t' do things if you move. Rock—turn around an' face the wall."

Rock did not delay this time; he turned around as Tad had directed. Tad stepped into the shack. He jerked Rock's gun out of its holster, shoved the weapon into his own belt. He looked at Riggs, then down at the gun at his feet. He lashed out suddenly, vicious, with his right foot, caught the gun squarely, and it spun across the room, collided with the wall, caromed off and slid over the floor and disappeared under the bunk. Riggs gave him a murderous glare.

"Back up," Tad ordered.

The muzzle of the Colt bored into Riggs' stomach and the man backed against the wall.

"Wanna warn you polecats that you're covered fr'm the outside, too," Tad said. He stepped to the window, yanked the shade hard. It shot upward, spun around the wooden roller wildly, noisily, for a minute, then it subsided. "Shorty! Poke th' snoot o' your rifle in here so's these buzzards c'n see it."

Cahill's thumping heart had quieted down. Now he was calm, and he was beginning to enjoy the little drama that he pushed the window up as far as it could go, then he rested the barrel on the sill. It gaped hungrily at the men in front of it.

"There y'are," Tad said. "If any o' you get 'ny ideas, take at look at that rifle b'fore you act up."

He backed toward the door, closed it behind him with a backward thrust of his leg, then he leaned back against the door. His eyes ranged over the room briefly.

"We-ll," he said presently. "Here we are at last. The end o' the trail f'r you three skunks. Bet none o' you ever dreamed you'd wind up this way, but it on'y goes t' show you that once you start buckin' fate, you're leadin' with your chin an' you're askin' f'r whatever you get. An' you fellers are sure gonna get it—b'lieve me! Y'know, I was gonna say a lotta things t' you fellers, but now I realize I'd be wastin' my breath, so th' hell with it. What I'm gonna say now is gonna be short an' to th' point, an' when I'm finished we'll all head out o' here, t'gether. Priddy, I ain't got 'ny sympathy f'r you. You got so damned big f'r your britches you thought you could get away with murder. This proves you can't. You're a double-barreled skunk, but you're lucky at that—lucky I came along even though I did spoil your plans. I went t' the trouble o' diggin' into things, an' because I did, your neck's saved. I found out that you didn't kill th' Hassetts even though you thought you did. An' I found out that Riggs an' his side partner were th' ones who did kill th' Hassetts. You didn't know that, did you?"

Priddy's mouth opened, his lower lip sagged as he stared at Tad. He closed his mouth clumsily, swallowed hard, tried to speak, but only a choking gurgling sound resulted. Tad glanced at Riggs but the man averted his eyes. Tad turned to Priddy again.

"You plugged both o' the Hassetts with your rifle," Tad went on. "You winged both o' them in the same place, right alongside the head. When you saw blood spout out, you were satisfied that you'd killed th'm. But you didn't kill th'm, Priddy. You wounded th'm, stunned th'm, and that's where Riggs an' Rocky took over. They musta known what you were up to, and why you were up to it. They finished the job you thought you did on the Hassetts, and they let you go on thinkin' you did it. Then they lay back f'r a spell, waitin' f'r you t' uncover the Hassett gold, figgerin' that when you got your hands on it, they'd be right b'hind you, offerin' t' split it with you or t' bluff you into thinkin' they'd squeal on you if you wouldn't cut them in. When they started t' walk outta here, that was on'y 'n act. They were just tryin' t' scare you into callin' thm back an', f'r all I know, maybe at th' last minute it would've worked."

He paused, looked at Riggs again. The foreman did not raise his eyes to meet Tad's. Instead he stared moodily and sullenly into space.

"That's th' story, Priddy," Tad said evenly. "I s'ppose I oughta tell you that th' Hassetts weren't shot t' death. They were knifed. I know b'cause a couple o' us dug up th' bodies an' looked th'm over."

There was a chuckle from Cahill and Tad looked at him quickly. Cahill swung himself up, settled himself astride the window sill.

"Aren't you going to tell Mr. Priddy about the gold?" he asked.

Tad grinned at him.

"I was savin' that f'r later on," he answered.

"This is as good a time as any," Cahill said, "to see Mister Priddy eat crow. I've waited a long time for that moment, so why put it off?"

"Awright," Tad said. "Here goes. Priddy, we found the Hassett strongbox. It was loaded t' the top. An' y'know what was in it? It was full o' little chunks o' rock an' shale, bright, shiny little pieces, but there wasn't 'n ounce o' gold in th' hull blamed box. Everybody knew they were loco. You did, too, and if you'da had 'ny sense you'da known they didn't know a nugget fr'm a hailstone."

There was no sound from Ben Priddy. For a long moment the shack was hushed. Then Cahill laughed long and hard.

"Let's go," Tad said finally. "Shorty, hustle aroun' outside f'r their horses, then go an' get ours. And if you find 'ny rope layin' around, bring it back with you. We're gonna need it."

CHAPTER FOURTEEN

Shorthorn was hushed and dark and asleep, and wrapped in deep shadows when Tad and Cahill pulled up at the entrance to the town.

"Here goes," Tad said as he dismounted. He tossed Mike's reins into his companion's hands, hitched up his pants. "Sit tight, partner. I won't be long."

"O-h, take your time," Cahill answered airily. "Pray do. After all, what's the loss of a night's sleep among friends? Nothing, nothing at all."

Tad grinned at him over his shoulder, then he strode away. Presently he mounted the sidewalk and the warped boards creaked and squealed under his boots. Cahill watched him. When he saw Tad turn into a darkened doorway, he dismounted, led the horses forward, then guided them across the road to the leaning signpost, tied them to it, then sauntered off. Unhurriedly he strolled along the street, stopped for a moment when he came to a dark alley, peered into it, then went on. When he came to the next alley he looked into it, smiled and trudged down its dark length. He reappeared a minute later astride a horse, and leading two others. Slowly he rode up the street, reined in at the signpost, dismounted again, and tethered the newly acquired horses alongside Mike and his own borrowed horse. He suddenly remembered that Tad had given him Rock's gun. He drew it out of his waistband, hefted it, fanned it, nodded to himself. He wheeled, snapped the gun upward, leveled it at an imaginary foe, pretended to snap a shot, jerked the gun upward and peered hard at his own shadow that fell across the ground.

"H'm," he said aloud. "Got the varmint first shot."

He wheeled again, leveled the gun here and there, backed a bit, dashed forward again, then he stopped and fanned the weapon. He looked up, found Mike eyeing him .... He frowned, shoved the gun into his waistband, pulled the brim of his hat down over his eyes, sauntered over to his horse and climbed into the saddle. He did not look at Mike; after a minute the mare made a strange noise. Cahill's head jerked up.

"Is that so?" he demanded. "We-ll, let me tell you something, my fine friend. I admit your Mister Cole is rather expert with his Colt, but after all these years, he should be. It's all a matter of practice, y'know, and doubtless he grew up with a Colt for a play-toy. I went in for the finer things in life, and Colts aren't rated in that category. But you may depend upon this—if I had had an opportunity to become acquainted with a six-gun and thus develop my skill with it, doubtless I too would have become equally proficient."

Mike had listened attentively; at least, she gave the appearance of having listened. Now she raised her head and emitted a sound that proved even more offensive to Cahill's ears. He stiffened with indignation.

"That, madam," he said very loftily, "is indication of low breeding. Let us consider our friendship at an end. Henceforth, when we meet, I shall ask you to maintain a polite silence. For my part, I shall ignore you completely. And now be good enough to turn your head the other way."

Judge Bailey and County Attorney Cummings were out of their beds by a prodding and definitely uncompromising Colt in the hands of Tad Cole. Bailey was a bit annoyed when he was awakened. He sputtered and mumbled a great deal about the sanctity of the law, but he finally got out of bed and into his clothes. Cummings displayed unusually good humor for such an early hour in the morning. Perhaps he realized the futility of arguing with a determined young man with a very business-like way of handling a gun. He got out of bed at once, dressed, stopped briefly when he was putting on his coat, looked at Tad, who, gun in hand, was leaning against the closed door of Cummings' room.

"You look vaguely familiar," he said finally.

"That so?"

"Yes. We've probably met somewhere."

"Could be. I've been places."

Judge Bailey was sitting in a far corner. He grunted and Cummings turned his head.

"This person," Bailey said with a trace of annoyance in his voice, "is the one responsible for that Walker boy's escape from court."

"Indeed!" Cummings said, and he looked at Tad again, then he smiled. "Then we did meet somewhere, didn't we?"

"Don't be an ass!" the judge said sharply.

"I hope you won't take offense at the judge's manner," Cummings said. "He isn't an early riser normally, and I'm afraid he won't be as congenial as usual until much later in the day. So you're the young man who cheated Ben Priddy out of a hanging! Well, well!"

"If you'll forgive me for interrupting this delightful tete-a-tete," Bailey said. "Will one of you be good enough to tell me why I was routed out of my bed at this unheard of hour of the night?"

"It isn't night any longer, Judge," Cummings said. "It's morning."

"That's quite beside the point!"

"I'm afraid I shall have to refer you to our young friend," Cummings said. "I'm pretty sure he can answer."

"Young man," Judge Bailey said sternly. "I warn you that you shall be held accountable for this night's work!"

Tad merely smiled.

"Now then," the judge went on, "just what is the meaning of this—this—"

Tad eyed him for a moment.

"Well?" Bailey demanded. "Answer me!"

"Anybody ever tell you t' shut up?" Tad countered.

Judge Bailey bounded to his feet.

"Young man!" he thundered, "how dare you?"

Tad did not answer. Instead, the muzzle of the Colt came up a bit. It gaped hungrily at Judge Bailey's stomach. The judge glared at Tad briefly, then his eyes went down, focused on the Colt's black mouth, and finally he grunted and sat down again.

"You open your mouth t' me again like you did," Tad said coldly, "an' I'll put my foot in it. If you think I'm kiddin', you try me. You, Cummings, step on it. We've got a ride ahead uv us an' it's gettin' later all th' time."

"I'm quite ready," Cummings announced.

"God," Tad said. "Now look. You fellers go out ahead o' me, but don't think you c'n pull anything an' get away with it. This Colt c'n get awf'lly nasty when it has to. Get it? Awright then. Up on your feet, Judge."

Minutes later Tad led his captives up to where Cahill was waiting.

"Here y'are, Shorty," Tad said. "They're all yours. Got that gun I gave you?"

"Yes, of course."

"We-ll, if either o' th'm tries 'nything, turn it loose on 'im."

"It will be a pleasure," Cahill answered. "Judge Bailey, Mister Cummings—"

"Please be assured that we have no intention of doing anything other than that which you direct," Cummings said quickly.

Tad grinned, turned on his heel and strode off again.

Waking Sheriff Blix Higgins proved considerably more difficult than the others. There was an empty whiskey bottle under Higgins' bed, and another on the floor near the door. Tad eyed them, made his way to the bed, bent over the sleeping man and shook him.

"Awright, Higgins," he said. "Haul your fat carcass outta that bed."

There was no response.

"Hey," Tad said loudly. "Wake up!"

Higgins grunted, turned over on his back. Tad went out of the room; he returned shortly with a bucket more than half filled with water.

"Get up, Higgins," he said. "Higgins!"

It was completely evident that the sheriff would not respond to normal methods. Tad stepped back a bit, raised the bucket, emptied it on the sprawled-out figure on the bed. Higgins awoke with a yell. Water dripped off his head and face. He forced himself upright, propped himself up on his wide-spread arms.

"Help!" he sputtered and he choked when water filled his throat. "Help, somebody! I'm drownin'!"

The muzzle of Tad's Colt was suddenly jammed hard against his ribs. Higgings gulped.

"Shut up," Tad commanded. "Get outta that bed and climb into your clothes."

"Huh? Yeah—sure."

"Step on it."

The sheriff kicked off the soggy covers, swung his tree-trunk legs over the side of the bed. His hat hung over one bed-post, his shirt on another. His pants and boots lay on the floor. He snatched up the hat, clapped it on his head, grabbed the shirt and put it on, fumbled with the buttons but finally managed to complete the buttoning. He got into his pants, pulled on his boots.

"Let's go," Tad ordered.

With Higgins marching a single step ahead of him, Tad and the burly lawman trudged up the street. Cahill, the Colt in his hand, backed his horse away from the signpost.

"Take that horse over there, Sheriff," he said, pointing to the animal with his gun. "Judge, Mister Cummings—mount, please."

Tad vaulted up astride Mike's back. He wheeled the mare.

"You take the lead, Shorty," he called. "Awright, you fellers, fall in b'hind Shorty. Let's go."

The troop loped away. Judge Bailey moved away from Higgins and the sheriff edged his mount close to Cummings'."

"Where are we goin'?" he asked out of the corner of his mouth. "What's this all about?"

"Don't ask me," the county attorney replied. "I was simply invited to come along and the Colt in the hand of the young man who extended the invitation cautioned me not to ask questions."

"I know," Higgins said. "But what d'you think's gonna happen when we get to wherever we're headed for?"

"Come, come, Higgins," Cummings answered briskly. "Why try to conjecture? Life can be awfully short, you know, so why not forget everything and concentrate on the cool beauty of the night and the surrounding countryside?"

The sheriff guided his horse away, rode on in silence.

It was nearly dawn when they clattered past the barn and pulled up at the Walkers' back door. As they dismounted, Eve appeared in the doorway.

"Oh!" she said quickly. She turned, spoke over her shoulder. "They're here, Dan."

She opened the door wide, held it for Judge Bailey and Vance Cummings. She smiled at Cahill, looked up at Tad who winked at her, and who squeezed her hand as he stepped inside. Priddy, Riggs and Rock, their hands bound behind them and their crossed ankles tied securely to the bottom rung of their chairs, sat in a row against the far wall. Dan and Curly Walker, their rifles laid across their knees, sat in opposite corners of the room.

"Hi," Dan said, and he got stiffly to his feet.

Judge Bailey stopped, looked at Priddy and the two men beside him, and frowned.

"What's the meaning of this?" he demanded. He turned and glared at Tad.

"You'll know soon enough," Tad replied. "But get this straight, Judge. This ain't one o' Priddy's crooked courtrooms, so don't put on 'n act f'r us. That clear? Dan, swing that chair around here, will you? Curly, be a good feller an' let Cummings have your chair."

Cummings nodded to Curly, moved forward, took the vacated chair and seated himself. The judge hesitated for a moment, then he sat down, too.

"Now, look," Tad said again. "I shouldn't hafta tell you fellers what t' do, but bein' that this is a mite irregular, I'm going to tell you what's what. We caught Priddy an' his two hired hands in one o' the Hassett's shack. We know who killed the Hassetts and why. You get the story fr'm the prisoners in your own way. That'll make it legal. When you're finished, and sentence is passed, the prisoners are yours. But b'fore you go, you, Cummings, you write out somethin' f'r Curly that'll tell the world he's free an' clear. The judge'll sign it. Now go ahead.

It was quiet in the barn where Mike and the family's remaining horse, a rawboned male, were munching some hay and grain. Mike glanced at her companion once or twice but each time she shook her head sadly. He would never take the place of the handsome gelding. Mike sighed deeply, but she did not permit her disappointment to interfere with her munching.

In the house it was quiet too. Tad and Eve, the only ones left, were in the kitchen; Tad astride a chair that he had tilted back against the wall, seemed to be in deep thought, while Eve was equally pensive and silent as she rolled out dough for a pie she had promised to bake for supper.

A conference following Riggs' reluctantly given confession of Rock's and his guilt had resulted in a decision to let Ben Priddy go free. Cummings, moved by Dan's willingness to let bygones be bygones, had suggested that, in view of the damage done by the Walkers, Priddy deed over to the Walkers one-third of his spread. Dan had countered with an offer to take over one-third of Priddy's indebtedness to the bank on condition that bank issue new and longer term notes for what Priddy owed it. Judge Bailey, a principal stockholder, had assured him the bank would do so. At his insistence, Dan agreed to accompany them to Shorthorn to complete the necessary arrangements and to sign the papers certifying to his part in the deal. Cahill had gone along in order to gather together his personal belongings and bring them back to the Walker place. As yet he preferred to delay his final decision about resuming the practice of medicine. He would work for Dan for a while, and then he would see what developed.

As for Riggs and Rock, Judge Bailey, sitting in supreme authority, had found them guilty of manslaughter and had sentenced them to spend the rest of their natural lives in prison. They were handed over to Higgins, who was instructed to deliver them to the prison keeper at Chadwick, some two hundred miles south of Shorthorn. They were hoisted into their saddles and, with Higgins' eye and a borrowed Colt on them, they started away on their last ride.

Last of all was Curly, although he had been the first to leave. He had pleaded with Tad to keep the judge there until he returned. And return he did, accompanied by Lila and her mother. Then, with Eve and Dan standing up for them, Curly and Lila were married by Judge Bailey. At Martha Priddy's urging, the young people had agreed to live with the Priddys. Curly had hesitated about it at first but Lila soon won her over. He would be given a "piece" of Priddy's spread, and their living would be assured. But now they too were gone. It had all been so sudden—so many things happening in such swift succession—but now it was over and nothing but faint echoes lingered about the place.

"I do hope Curly will be happy," Eve said suddenly. "He's only a boy, you know, and I can't get used to the idea that he's married."

"You haven't had time yet," Tad answered. "But he'll be awright. I'm sure uv it."

"I hope so," Eve said with a sigh.

"An' don't you go worryin' about him an' Priddy gettin' along. The wind's been knocked outta ol' Ben an' he'll never be th' same ornery cuss he used t' be. Then one o' these days the ranch'll b'long t' the kids and they'll be ridin' high."

Eve's answer took the form of another sigh.

Presently Tad's chair came down on all four legs. He got to his feet, stretched himself, hitched up his belt and sauntered to the door, opened it and idled in the doorway.

"Gee," he said, finally, "it's sure quiet around here. Don't seem like th' same place."

He leaned against the door frame, lapsed into thoughtful silence. After a while Eve turned and looked at him.

"Tad."

"Huh? You sayin' somethin'?"

"What are you thinking about?"

"O-h, nothing in p'rticular."

"Don't you want to tell me?"

"I was just thinkin' about home. That's all."

"I see."

She did not press him. Instead she waited for him to continue.

"You've never seen Kansas," he mused shortly. "You've sure missed somethin'. Ain't 'ny place in the hull world just like it. It's big an' clean an' everything that grows there is just about the best you c'n find anywhere. That's a fact. Then you oughta see our place. Heck, I'll bet you could put Priddy's spread in one corner an' never know it was there. You ever see wheat in th' mornin' sun, or f'r that matter, around early evening when th' sun's set-tlin' down away off in the distance? It looks like gold, Eve, miles an' miles uv it, or as far as you c'n see. It just about takes your breath away. No kiddin'."

Eve did not interrupt his thoughts.

"You'd like it there," he went on again. "I know you would. Got th' nicest folks all around us. I've know th'm all since I was knee-high to a grasshopper."

"You're homesick, Tad."

"O-h, I dunno."

"Then what is it?"

He did not answer immediately.

"You can tell me, Tad," she urged.

"He straightened up, hitched up his belt again, turned and came striding across the room.

"Awright," he said. "I will."

She bent over the dough and the other things, for she dared not raise her eyes.

Then he was standing beside her.

"Eve," he said.

"Y-yes?"

"The other night. Did you mean that?"

"Did I mean what?"

"Look," he said a bit impatiently. "D'you suppose you c'n forget about that blamed pie f'r a minute an kinda look up at me while I'm talkin' t' you?"

"You want pie, don't you?"

"Sure, on'y there's somethin' else I want a heap more'n I do pie."

Slowly she raised her head. Her face was flushed.

"That's better," he said. "I asked you b'fore, did you mean that the other night?"

"And I said, did I mean what?"

His lips tightened and tiny red patches danced into his cheeks.

"When you kissed me!" he almost yelled. "That's what!"

"You needn't shout at me, Tad Cole," she said indignantly. "The whole world doesn't have to hear you. As for kissing you, I think it was just the other way around. As I recall it, you kissed me."

"Awright," he said. "Awright, I kissed you. That better?"

"Much better," she said loftily.

"Then that part's settled. I kissed you. Swell. Then you kissed me back. All I wanna know is, did you mean it?"

Her eyes were wide and starry and soft.

"Did you mean it, Tad?"

"Danged right I did! What d'you think I am, huh? One o' them fellers who goes aroun' kissin girls an'—"

"I'm glad you meant it. I wondered about it."

"You don't haft wonder 'nymore. You know. Now what about it?"

"What about what, Tad?"

"F'r Pete's sake, Eve," he sputtered. "You know what I mean. I'm askin' you t' marry me. What'd you think I was talkin' about?"

"O-h!" she said inadequately.

"What do I hafta do? Make a pretty speech an' tell you how beautiful you are an' all that kind o' thing?"

"Am I beautiful, Tad?"

"An' how you are!"

"What else am I, Tad?"

"You're doggoned sweet, that's what you are! You've got everything, fr'm looks t' guts, an' there ain't a girl here or any-where else that c'n hold a candle t' you."

"You're sweet too, Tad."

"Yeah, sure. Look, you gonna marry me or not—huh?"

"Don't you think the matter of love should be considered?"

"Are you kiddin'?" he demanded. "Ever since th' other night I've been walkin' around in circles. What d'you think that came fr'm, somethin' I ate?"

"I don't know, Tad," she said innocently.

"You don't, hey? Then I'll tell you, doggone it. You did it. Maybe I've been in love with you fr'm the very beginning. Chances are I was, on'y I was too danged dumb t' know it. But the other night I found out f'r sure and in heck uva hurry, too, and I've been moonin' around ever since."

She laughed softly. He bent quickly and kissed her lips, stilled her laughter.

"Eve," he said huskily.

She came to him willingly and his arms encircled her. She raised her head, then she reached up, drew his head down and kissed him. Her arms tightened around his neck.

"Hey," he said suddenly.

"What is it?" she asked anxiously.

"How soon d'you suppose we could leave here?"

"Why, as soon as you like."

"Swell. Look, you get ready while I go get the horses. We'll ride into town an' have Judge Bailey marry us. Awright?"

"But what about the pie?"

"Pie?" he echoed. "F'rget it! You've got th' rest o' your life t' make me pies, so I reckon I c'n pass up this one! G'wan now! Step on it!"